This is the first book of saga about an English serf who rose to become the captain of a company of English archers and forever changed England. It was prepared for an unknown benefactor by the monks of the Priory of St. Frideswide in Oxford, the monastery Wolsey dissolved and Henry the Eighth subsequently re-founded as the College of Christ Church after he broke with Rome. The other books in this exciting medieval saga about an English serf who rose and lived and loved in rough and dangerous medieval England during the years prior to the Magna Carta are also available on Kindle. They can all be found as eBooks on Amazon, and many of them are available in print. Search for *Martin Archer fiction*.

The parchments on which the stories in this saga are based were found some years ago in a trunk buried under a pile of rubble in the Bodelian Library basement. The monks' assignment was to translate and piece together what was left of numerous earlier records and parchments into one great history of the Norman kingdom of England similar to the history Livy wrote for Rome so many years ago—with its emphasis on using the various participants' own words to describe what they were thinking and doing during the events which shaped Rome.

Among the many problems the unknown author of the parchments said he had to overcome was the problem that the exciting tales in the parchments contained so many surprises and often had missing parts where the mice had eaten the parchment.

What follows in this particular novel, the first of the books in the saga, was mostly taken from the parchments describing the adventures and battles of William, the serf from Kent who rose in the years after King Richard's crusade to become the captain of what was left of a company of English archers. Other sources were parchments from other scribes describing the activities and thoughts of William's priestly brother Thomas, his son George, and several of William's key lieutenants and sergeants.

The position of the Church and the Crown has always been that the changes that William and his company of archers caused in Medieval England and the Holy Land were "God's Will." The monks were obviously not so sure—their accounts and the descriptions and explanations of the people involved suggested strong arms, longbows and bladed pikes, and determined men were a much more likely explanation.

Only one thing is absolutely certain—men haven't changed much at all since the brutal days of medieval England.

The Archers

Chapter One

Captain William

The weary men straggled out of the mountains and into the Syrian port of Latika late in the morning. There were eighteen of them, all English archers, and most of them had walked day and night for the past three days. The only exceptions were two wounded men on a makeshift litter being dragged behind a dusty camel and a brown-robed priest riding on an exhausted horse and holding a sleeping young boy. The boy was being held inside the priest's robe to protect him against the chill of the spring day. They were all that remained of a company of one hundred and ninety two archers who had sailed with King Richard when he abandoned his people and lands to go crusading.

******

I was walking at the front of the column and stopped and waited until the priest reached me.

"How's George?" I asked the priest.

I gestured with a tired wave of his hand towards the sleeping child as I asked.

"Your son is fine, William," answered the priest as the horse stopped.

The boy woke up at the sound of the voices and twisted around to get more comfortable in the priest's arms when the horse stopped. Then he sat up straight and looked around.

"Put me down, Uncle Thomas, I want to walk with my father and the men for a while. My arse is sore and I'm thirsty."

And with a little twist, the boy wriggled out of the priest's arms and the robe and slid off the horse before the priest could even answer. He was barefoot and wearing a rough brown shirt which hung to his knees. Edward the tailor had sewn it for him before he'd been killed by an unlucky stone that had been catapulted over the wall by the Saracens and had hit him on the head.

"Look, Uncle Thomas, what is it?"

The boy asked the question of the priest as he massaged his rear with one hand and with the other pointed to the flat grey expanse of the Mediterranean spreading out beyond the stone houses and the boats in the harbour.

"It's a very big lake with water so salty you can't drink it. Those things out there float on top of the water are the big boats called cogs and they carry people across the big lake just like the boats on a river can carry people across the river. The only difference is those you see out there can carry more people and have much bigger sails."

The boy was not convinced as he stood there studying the boats.

"They look little."

"They'll look bigger when we get closer."

"Really?"

The boy looked intensely at the scene in front of him. Then he shook his head and looked back at his father questioningly.

"Your uncle is right, George. All of us can fit on one of those cogs with room to spare. The big ones can carry as many as two hundred men or even more. Your uncle and I and all the archers came here from England on cogs just like those.

Almost a hundred of us came on each cog. And sailing on one of them is how we'll go back—all together."

Except, I thought, we've got to collect the coins we are owed so we'll be able to pay a cog or boat to carry us away from this place, and there will only be eighteen of us instead of the one hundred and ninety-two who came out from England with King Richard seven years ago—and it will be eighteen only if we can get the arrow out of Brian's leg without it rotting and Athol stops getting dizzy and falling down whenever he tries to walk.

I didn't tell George that we had no way to buy our passage out of this place unless the Bishop paid us the bezant gold coins Lord Edmund contracted to pay us for defending his lands for the past two years. Well, we'll know soon enough, won't we?

Walking down the hill to the port took us the better part of an hour. We followed the dirt trail down the hill to the low-walled caravanserai where the men of the caravans and their horses and livestock lived outside Latika's city walls. It was a cool, early spring day on the Syrian coast.

******

We had heard the city was packed with Christians and Jews fleeing the oncoming Saracens and that the city gates were closed to the refugees because there were so many of them. One look and we could see the rumour was true. Even at a distance we could smell the people and their livestock and see the clouds of dust they were raising.

Shouts and many great cries went up as the people standing and sitting around the city gate saw us walking in. They knew what our arrival meant. It meant Lord Edmund's crusader castle and lands in the mountain pass between Damascus and the coast had been lost and the Saracens were coming.

It also meant, at best, that these people will either have to convert to Islam or die; and most likely they'd all be put to the sword or taken away as slaves. And so would we if the Bishop of Damascus didn't pay us so we could get away or ransom ourselves to freedom.

The caravanserai master himself, a great bearded man with long grey hair, came to his gate with several armed retainers as we came closer, and the shouting and weeping crowd grew around us with their desperately shouted questions and reaching hands. He looked over my little column and then at me with a baleful eye as I stopped in front of him with George holding my hand.

"So it is true? Lord Edmund and the castle have finally fallen?"

"Aye, they have; the road to Damascus is open."

The caravanserai master crossed himself.

"Well, everyone needs a caravanserai so I guess I'll be a Moslem again until the Christians or Jews come back. But these people," he said as he shook his head in resignation and gestured both towards the people gathering around us and the distant crowds, "I just don't know."

Well I know; anyone who stays here will either be slaughtered or become a Moslem slave. That's why we left four days ago when Lord Edmund fell.

"Do you know the whereabouts of the Bishop of Damascus? We heard he's fled to here. We have a message for him."

"He's in the city at the Church of Saint Mary."

Then the caravanserai master gestured at the crowd again and shook his head in disgust and resignation, and added something chilling.

"But you better hurry if you want to see him. I've heard he's about to run off and leave us."

To make matters worse, he then gave us even more bad news.

"We are full here. I have no room left inside. If you bring me a copper coin, you can send someone in to fetch water from my well—but you and your men and their weapons must stay outside."

******

I decided to leave George with Randolph to guard him while my brother Thomas and I went to see the Bishop to get our pay—four bezant gold coins from Constantinople for each man. Quite a bit for only two years of service, but we'd paid dearly for it by so many of us losing our lives.

At least we tried to see the Bishop. The guards at the city gate would not let us in even though Thomas is a priest.

One of the guards looked a little bit smarter and greedier than the other two. Thomas motioned him aside and blessed him. I watched as they huddled together for a moment talking in low voices.

Then Thomas waved me over.

"William, this good man can't leave his post to tell the Bishop we are here. And it's a pity for we only need to see His Eminence for a few minutes to deliver an important message.

"It's a problem we need to solve because it wouldn't be a Christian thing to make someone as important as the good Bishop upset. He's sure to be unhappy if he has to walk all this way just to have a word with us."

"Ah. I understand. The guard wants a bribe to let us in.

"Let us in and you and the others can come with us when we sail away from here," I said.

"Forget it, English. I've got a wife and family here. I am not going anywhere."

It was time to take another tack. I reached into my almost empty purse and pulled out two small copper coins—enough for a night of drinking if the wine is bad enough. I pressed them into his grimy hand.

"We only need a few minutes to deliver a message. We'll be out and gone before anyone knows."

The guard looked at the coins and then again at us, sizing us up was what he was doing, and he didn't like what he saw. We looked like what we were, poor and bedraggled.

"One more copper. There are three of us on duty and no one is supposed to enter. But we'll take a chance, since it's for the Bishop and our sergeant is not here."

I agreed with a sigh and dug out another copper.

"We won't be long and the Bishop will appreciate it." *No, he won't.*

Thomas waved the wooden cross he wore around his neck to bless the guard as he put our coppers in his purse, and then he waved it at the other two for good measure.

******

Thomas and I had to shoulder our way through the crowded streets and push people away as we walked towards the church. Beggars and desperate women and young boys began pulling on our clothes and crying out to us. In the distance black smoke was rising from somewhere in the city, probably from looters torching somebody's house or shop.

The doors to the front of the church were barred. Through the cracks in the wooden doors we could see the big wooden bar holding them shut.

"Come on. There must be a side door for the priests to use. There always is."

We walked around to the side of the church and there it was. I began banging on the door. After a while, a muffled voice on the other side told us to go away.

"Go away. The church is not open."

"We've come from Lord Edmund to see the Bishop of Damascus. Let us in."

We could hear something being moved and then an eye appeared at the peep hole in the door. A few seconds later, the door swung open and we hurried in.

The light inside the room was dim because the windows were shuttered.

Our greeter was a slender fellow with alert eyes who couldn't be much more than an inch or two over five feet tall. He studied us intently as he bowed us in and then quickly shut and barred the door behind us. He seemed quite anxious.

"We've come from the Bekka Valley to see the Bishop," I said in the bastardised French dialect some are now calling English. And then Thomas repeated my words in Latin. *Which, of course, is what I should have done in the first place.*

"I shall tell His Eminence that you are here and ask if he will receive you," the man replied in Latin. "I am Yoram, the Bishop's scrivener; may I tell him who you are and why you are here?"

"I am William, the captain of what's left of a company of English archers, and this is Father Thomas, our priest. We are here to collect our pay for helping to defend Lord Edmund's fief these past two years."

"I shall inform His Eminence of your arrival. Please wait here."

The Bishop' scrivener had a strange accent; I wondered where he came from?

Some time passed before the anxious little man returned. While he was gone we looked around the room. It was quite luxurious with a floor of stones instead of the mud floors one usually finds in churches.

It was also quite dark. The windows were covered with heavy wooden shutters and sealed shut with heavy wooden bars; the light in the room, such as it was, came from cracks in the shutters and smaller windows high on the walls above the shuttered windows. There was a somewhat tattered tribal carpet on the floor.

The anxious little man returned and gave us a most courteous nod and bow.

"His Grace will see you now. Please follow me."

The Bishop's clerk led us into a narrow, dimly lit passage with stone walls and a low ceiling. He went first and then Thomas and then me. We'd taken but a few steps when he turned back toward us and in an intense low voice issued a terse warning.

"Protect yourselves. The Bishop doesn't want to pay you. You're in mortal danger."

The little man nodded in silent agreement when I held up my hand. Thomas and I needed to take a moment to get ourselves ready.

His eyes widened and he watched closely as we prepared. Then, when I gave a nod to let him know we were ready, he rewarded us with a tight smile and another nod—and began walking again with a particularly determined look on his face.

A few seconds later we turned another corner and came to an open wooden door. It opened into a large room with beamed ceilings more than six feet high and stone walls begrimed by centuries of smoke. I knew the height because I could stand upright after I bent my head to get through the entrance door.

A portly middle-aged man in a bishop's robes was sitting behind a table covered with parchments and there was a bearded and rather formidable-looking guard with a sword in a wooden scabbard standing in front of the table on our side of it. There was a closed chest on the table sitting on some of the parchments and a jumble of tools and chests in the corner covered by another old tribal rug and a broken chair.

The Bishop smiled to show us his bad teeth and beckoned us in. We could see him clearly despite the dim light coming in from the small window openings near the ceiling of the room.

After a moment he stood and extended his hand over the table so we could kiss his ring. First Thomas and then I approached and half kneeled to kiss it. Then I stepped back and towards the guard to make room for Thomas so he could re-approach the table and stand next to me as the Bishop re-seated himself.

"What is it you want to see me about?" the Bishop asked in Latin.

He said it with a sincere smile and leaned forward expectantly.

"I am William, captain of the late Lord Edmund's company of English archers, and this is Father Thomas, our priest and confessor." *And my older brother, though I don't think I will mention it at the moment.*

"How can that be? Another man was commanding the archers when I visited Lord Edmund earlier this year, and we made our arrangements."

"He is dead. He took an arrow in the arm and it turned purple and rotted until he died. Another took his place and now he's dead also. Now I am the captain of the company."

The Bishop crossed himself and mumbled a brief prayer under his breath. Then he looked at me expectantly and listened intently.

"We've come to get the money Lord Edmund entrusted to you to pay us. We looked for you before we left the valley, but

Beaufort Castle was about to fall and you'd already gone. So we've come here to collect our pay."

"Of course. Of course. I have it right here in the chest.

"Aran," he said, nodding to the burly soldier standing next to me, "tells me there are eighteen of you. Is that correct?" *And how would he be knowing that?*

"Yes, Eminence, that is correct."

"Well then, four gold Constantinople coins for each man is seventy-two; and you shall have them here and now."

"No, Eminence, that is not correct."

I reached inside my jerkin and pulled out the company's copy of the contract with Lord Edmund, laid the parchment on the desk in front of him, and turned it around so he could read the words in Latin that had been scribed on it and see Edmund's mark.

As I placed the contract on the table, I tapped it with my finger and casually stepped further to the side, and even closer to his swordsman, so Thomas could once again step into my place in front of the Bishop and nod his agreement, confirming it was indeed in our contract.

"The contract calls for four gold bezant coins from Constantinople for each of one hundred and twenty-three men and two more coins to the company for each man who is killed or loses both of his eyes or his bollocks. It sums to one thousand and twenty-six bezants in all—and I know you have our money because I was present when Lord Edmund gave you many more coins and you agreed to pay them to us. We are here to collect our bezants."

"Oh yes. So you are. So you are. Of course. Well, you shall certainly get what is due you. God wills it."

I sensed the swordsman stiffen as the Bishop said the words and opened the lid of the chest. The Bishop reached in with both hands and took a big handful of bezants in his left hand and placed them on the table.

He spread the gold coins out on the table and motioned Thomas forward to help him count as he reached back in to fetch another handful. I stepped further to the left and even closer to the guard so Thomas would have plenty of room to step forward to help the Bishop count.

Everything happened at once, when Thomas leaned forward to start counting the coins. The Bishop reached again into his money chest as if to get another handful. This time he came out with a dagger—and lunged across the coins on the table to drive it into Thomas's chest with a grunt of satisfaction.

The swordsman next to me simultaneously began pulling his sword from its wooden scabbard. It had all been prearranged.

A look of surprise and amazement appeared on the Bishop's face when his dagger was turned aside by the chain mail Thomas always wear under his priest's cassock. It disappeared an instant later when Thomas pushed the knife he'd been holding in his hand under his robe straight into the Bishop's left eye. It slid in almost to the hilt.

The big guard went down before his sword cleared his scabbard. I used the knife I always carry in the leather sheath on my left wrist. I'd stopped to make sure it and its companion on my right wrist were in position when the Bishop's clerk warned us trouble was coming. Thomas had done the same with the wrist knives he always wears under his robe.

The Bishop's guard made two mistakes. He thought we would be intimidated by his fierce appearance and he had been gulled by watching my right hand as it rested carelessly on the handle of my sheathed sword. He also thought he was ready to strike and I was not.

All it had taken after I had moved closer to him to make way for Thomas was a snapped straightening of my bent left arm as the Bishop pulled his blade out of the box of coins and lunged at Thomas's heart.

My knife came out of my sleeve and went through the guard's beard and into his throat in the blink of an eye. He was very surprised. Yes he was. I could tell because I saw the flash of astonishment and panic in his eyes as he watched my hand streak towards him and felt the blade of the knife as I pushed it in.

I let loose of the handle and stepped back to watch impassively as the big man grabbed at my knife with both hands and tried to pull it out. He succeeded and great spurts of blood began when he got it out. He half-turned toward the Bishop with a look of imploring disbelief, and then back to look at me as he dropped my blade to the floor.

He was still looking at me with disbelieving eyes when he slowly sank to his knees and rocked back on to his heels with his hands clasping his throat in a desperate effort to stop the bleeding. That's where he died.

It was actually sort of strange how he died—he never fell over; he just stopped gasping and the light went out of his eyes. He died sitting back on his heels and that's where he stayed without falling over. I'd seen many a man die, but never one that ended up like that.

"Aren't you glad I made you practise with your wrist knives over and over again when you were a boy?"

That was my priestly brother's only comment as he jerked his blade out of the Bishop's eye and reached across the table for the chest.

He didn't look at me as he said it and he wasn't distracted by the vibrating spasms in the Bishop's legs as he finished his dying—he was too busy grabbing one corner of the chest and swinging it around so he could look in.

"Yes, Thomas, I am."

We both ignored the rattling *tap, tap, tap* as the Bishop's legs continued to tremble and kick one of the table legs.

******

The late Bishop's scrivener stood quietly in the corner. He had, and rightly so under the circumstances, a definite look of concern on his ashen face. He seemed to be quite agitated but trying hard to contain it. *Well, he certainly has nothing to fear from us.*

"Thank you, my friend," I said rather gently, with a gesture towards the dying Bishop. "Your warning saved us and we are much obliged to you. Will you be safe?"

"I hope so; I just don't know. But what about you—what will you and your men do now? How will you escape this place?"

"We'll try to hire a fishing boat or perhaps we'll walk down the coast to Acre before summer comes and it gets too hot. There are eighteen of us so we'll be hard to stop."

After a moment of thinking, I added something I've never once regretted.

"And why don't you come with us? We can always use a clerk and scrivener, especially an honest one who is a friend."

Our new friend didn't hesitate.

"Yes, I think I'd like to join you. I need to get out of here before the Saracens arrive and I was already planning to ask if I could leave with you. My name is Yoram, by the way. I am from a village near Damascus."

"Welcome to you, Yoram from Damascus. I am William, the captain of what is left of our company of English archers, and the ugly priest over there gathering up our money is my older brother, Thomas."

I named my brother ugly with a smile on my face and a great deal of affection. If it hadn't been for Thomas coming home to get me when he left the monastery to go on his crusade, I wouldn't have seen Jerusalem and he wouldn't have been able to teach me to read and write Latin and do my sums.

Where would I be? I'd still be in Kent and working from dawn till dusk on the little farm my father and mother worked as Lord Ansel's serfs until God took them when everyone but me died of the spotted pox.

And if I had stayed in Kent I would never have come to the Holy Land and tumbled the smith's daughter in Damascus who birthed my son before she died.

Yoram promptly knelt in front of me and put my foot on his head.

"Thank you, Captain William, I accept you as my liege lord and will serve you well."

Good grief, I have a vassal; I've never had one of those before.

"Uh. Yes. That is good. I accept you. Now stand up and tell me what you think. How best can we get back to our men from here with our coins? Who will try to stop us?"

"The two priests of the church are away. They were collecting coins in the villages between here and Beirut for the prayers needed to guard us against the Saracens. But there are three more of the Bishop's men outside napping in the walled garden behind the church. Only one of them is dangerous, My Lord."

My Lord?

Yoram thought for a moment, and then he added something important that forever changed my life.

"The other two might be useful to help us carry the money chests. The third is like Anil there; he'll either have to be killed or sent away on an errand."

"Chests? Are there more chests?"

"Yes, of course, Lord. Four more big ones in addition to the chest on the table. The Bishop has been collecting coins and jewels for more than two years to buy prayers to save the Christians from the Saracens.

"Everyone was told the Bishop was sending their donations to Rome to buy the prayers needed to save us. But he wasn't sending them—he was going to take them to the Pope himself and use them to buy himself an appointment in Rome. I know—I scribed the parchments because his hand was so poor."

"Where are they?" I asked. "The other chests, I mean?"

"Over there in the corner under the old rug with the shovels and hoe. He was afraid to let them out of his sight.

"That's why we are still here, isn't it? I arranged for a passage to Rome, but the captain of the cog I hired got terribly ill with some kind of pox whilst the Bishop was waiting for more coins and jewels to arrive.

"We were waiting for him to recover. But I am not sure we'd have gone even if the captain recovered."

After a pause, Yoram tried to explain.

"The Bishop meant well at first but he got overbalanced by his greed when we were forced to leave Damascus and then Beaufort—he not only wanted even more coins so he could buy a great position from the Pope, but he worried about his guards killing him and stealing them. He also thought the captain and the cog's crew would take them from him if his guards didn't."

Thomas and Yoram watched as I walked over and pulled the rugs off the chests. Four more chests. And they were heavy, yes they were. I tried to lift one and could barely get it off the ground. *God in heaven; we'll be rich if we get away with these.*

"We'll need a wain or cart," I announced to no one in particular. "And preferably a horse or donkey to pull it. We can say we need it to carry our two wounded men."

Thomas approved.

"Ah, now that's smart, that is. George can ride on it too."

I thought about our situation for a minute.

We'll need something to carry them with, and we might as well find out now if Yoram's oath is good.

"Yoram, here is what I want you to do."

******

My new vassal took the six gold bezants Thomas handed him from the pile on the Bishop's table, put them quite primly into a little leather purse, and slipped out the door. Thomas restored the door's big wooden bar as soon as it closed behind him.

After the door was barred, I pissed in the corner of the room while Thomas searched the bodies of the Bishop and his guard for weapons. He found nothing more but now, at least, we both had swords and I still had my longbow and eleven iron-tipped shafts.

And, of course, we now had a couple of additional daggers. The Bishop's was quite fine with little designs scratched into the handle.

Yoram's first stop was to visit the Bishop's remaining three guards and send the one he thought to be dangerous up the coast to Beirut to find another captain willing to carry the Bishop to Rome.

The dangerous guard was given four gold bezants by Yoram and told to go to Beirut and offer them to the captain of the first cog or galley he could find who was willing to come to Latika to fetch the bishop—with the promise of sixty more for one voyage to carry the Bishop and five retainers to Rome.

Yoram told us he thought the guard would disappear with the gold coins and never be heard from again. I wasn't sure; I thought he'd be swayed by all the coins in the Bishop's coin chests and the relative safety of Rome, and return with some kind of galley or cog, or even a big fishing boat with a sail.

In fact, we didn't care what the man did—it didn't matter so long as he wasn't here to try to stop us and the church's priests stayed away until we were long gone. If the dangerous guard didn't go, we'd have to kill him. The priests also if they returned before we left, unless they wanted to go with us.

******

It was all arranged. As soon as the guard left with the four gold bezants, Yoram would go to the market of the livestock traders in the field next to the caravanserai and buy the best horse and wagon he could find for two bezants or less. For such valuable coins he should be able to find a good horse and wagon and get some coppers and silvers back as well.

Best of all, he could tell the horse traders the truth—the English archers need them to carry their two wounded men and their captain's young son. No one would think we also needed them to carry chests of coins.

From the horse market, Yoram was to go to our camp next to the caravanserai with the horse and wagon and tell the men what they were to do.

The archers and all our possessions, including George and the horse and the wounded men on the camel litter, were to casually assemble outside the city gate in case they needed to rush in to help us fight our way out—or if we came out fast and need to run for it.

If he could bring them through the gate on our new horse cart, Yoram was to bring two or three of our sword-carrying archers back with him to help us load the chests and guard them. If he couldn't get the archers past the guards, he was to leave them at the gate and bring the horse and wagon by himself.

I gave Yoram one of my arrows so the men would know he came from me and told him not to mention the coin chests to the archers or anyone else, only that they must be standing by near the city gate for a rescue or to run for it.

After Yoram left and I put the bar back across the door, I was surprised to hear Thomas wanting to take some of the Bishop's other things with us—all the blank parchments in the room and the Bishop's gown, mitre, and crozier.

****** *William*

Time passed slowly, and Thomas and I got more and more anxious for Yoram to return. We both drew our swords and instinctively pulled down the sleeves on our robes to hide our daggers when we finally heard footsteps approach.

A few seconds later there was a quiet knock on the door and Yoram softly announced himself. Through a crack between the boards in the low wooden door, we could see him in the corridor. Several of our archers were standing behind him with their swords drawn.

Thomas opened the door quickly and let everyone in. They sensed the urgency and entered fast. Then Thomas restored the bar to prevent anyone else from getting in.

Yoram had brought Bob the Farmer and Long Bob from Chester with him, and he quickly announced, almost breathlessly, that there was another archer at the side door with the horse and wagon he'd bought.

"It's Andrew, the brewer, we've left guarding the wagon," Long Bob said as he stared at the bodies of the Bishop and his kneeling guard.

"I brought three of your men, the ones I saw with swords," explained Yoram anxiously.

"We didn't have any trouble at all passing through the city gate. I just drove up and waved to the men at the gate as we rode in on the wagon with one of your men driving the horse. They know me as the Bishop's man and didn't think anything of it. We left the rest of your men and the boy warming themselves in the sun just outside the city gate."

/At this point the parchment reached a ragged end, probably mice, so the scribe periodically had to use a sentence or two from Yoram's description of what happened to put together this part of William's tale./

Captain William thought for a moment and then he thanked me for doing a good job and began issuing orders. He told Father Thomas and me and the two Bobs to carry one of the rugs, the Bishop's chair, and one of the chests out to wagon.

Later, Captain William explained to me that putting the Bishop's broken chair and some ragged rugs on the wagon was not what anyone would expect to see on a wagon coming out of the city with chests of coins.

"Thomas, you best stay out there with Andrew Brewer to drive away the beggars and act priestly in case someone gets nosy.

"Yoram, you go with Thomas and begin carrying things to the wagon. Come back with the two Bobs as soon as possible to fetch the other coin chests and the big stack of blank parchment sheets on the table."

Then Captain William added, "And don't anyone act excited and move too fast; act bored, as if you're just doing a meaningless chore and nothing important is happening.

"I'll wait here with the guard's sword and the door barred in case anyone shows up."

I didn't know why but, as Father Thomas insisted, we took the big stack of parchments and the Bishop's writing materials and seal as well as the ring from his finger and the robes hanging on the peg by the door.

Captain William suddenly remembered something else.

"Wait." He held up a hand.

"Yoram," he told me with a disgusted shake of his head, "I forgot about the other two guards. Before you do anything else, go out back and check to make sure the one you think is a trouble maker is gone. Don't do anything if he's still here; just come back and tell me—so we can invite him in for a talk and kill him.

"If he's gone you can give the other two guards a choice—they can either carry out the Bishop's new orders and immediately go off to meet one of the church's priests and help guard the money he is bringing to the Bishop, or they can leave the Bishop's service and escape the Saracens by taking service with us.

"Tell them you have decided to go with us because you think the Bishop is coming down with smallpox. Also tell them the Bishop's guard, the dead one over there, Anil, I think you said his name was, just ran off to flee from the Bishop's pox.

"But whatever you do, don't let them in here to see the bodies. Take them around the church and in the side door if they want to pledge their liege and join us."

Yoram and Thomas smiled; the two Bobs looked confused.

******

The loading of the wagon went rapidly and we soon had all five of the coin chests and various other things in the wagon bed and covered with some of the dirty rags and the two ragged rugs. The tools and chair were stacked on top of them.

Walking down the street and leaving through the city gate turned out to be as easy as roasting a duck. Yoram and

Thomas rode on the horse-drawn wagon and the rest of us walked alongside of it.

The Bishop's two guards came with us. They kneeled before me and pledged their liege in the front room by the door where we'd first met Yoram.

Getting out of the city turned out to not be a problem at all.

It was the middle of a somewhat chilly early spring day and the guards were all out in the sun sitting against the side of the city wall to stay warm. They didn't even look up as our horse and wagon slowly clattered past and went out the gate.

No one except the beggars paid the slightest bit of attention to us and even the beggars didn't notice our bows were strung.

All our archers were standing or squatting on their heels near the city gate on the sunny side of the wall waiting for us. Everyone was near the gate and looked to be casually lounging about. Brian and Athol were on the camel litter, and Thomas was mounted on the horse and holding George. They were pointed away from gate in case we had to run.

Everything looked quite relaxed and normal. Randolph from London was the most ready of all—he had his sword unsheathed and was intensely studying it as he industriously rubbed it with sand as if to clean off some rust and grime.

Only someone who looked closely would have noticed each of the archers was wearing a couple of quivers and holding a bow already strung, and his hands were free so he could start pushing out arrows in an instant.

Raymond the ox herder from the village where the Thames can be forded, our best rider—*the only archer who really knew how to ride a horse*—was standing nearest to the gate. Everyone else was right around the corner next to our two wounded men—ready to grab them off the litter and throw them on the wagon if we needed to run for it.

Raymond was the first to see us as we approached the city gate to leave. He obviously said something to the others when he did. They all stood up and stretched and picked up their sleeping rolls and goods as we approached. No one hurried or appeared to be anxious.

I lifted a hand to give them a casual greeting as I led the horse around the corner so the guards could no longer see it or the wagon it was pulling.

George and our wounded men were promptly lifted aboard the wagon, Raymond took the horse's lead from me, and the men casually threw their personal things on the wagon as if it was something they did every day. Everyone looked relaxed and no one paid any attention to us. It took only a few seconds and no one on the crowded street paid us any attention, not even the beggars and street children. They'd already been waved away.

We slowly legged it back to the caravanserai as if we didn't have a care in the world—and then had to find a new place further from the caravanserai gate because our old one had already been taken by a couple of tents belonging to a merchant escaping from the interior with his family and servants.

And it was just as well we had to move. We didn't want anyone camping near enough to us to see what we had on our wagon.

I walked along side of the wagon and spoke with Yoram as we searched for a new place to camp.

"This sea captain whose cog the Bishop was going to use to escape. What's wrong with him?"

"He's got fevers and weakness from the French pox and doesn't want to leave his barber until he's cured. The barber is

bleeding him and has him drinking some kind of herbal tea
every two hours and eating some kind of paste made from
flowers, which makes him dream all the time and feel no pain."

"Let's go see him. Maybe I can convince him to change
his mind."

Chapter Two

Yoram the scribe

My new lords, Captain William and Father Thomas, settled the
archers in a new camp some distance away from the
caravanserai where it was less crowded. Then we walked
around the edge of the city wall and down to the harbour to
find the poxed captain.

The captain brought little George with us and four of the
archers for protection—Randolph, the two Bobs, and
Raymond. He let George ride on his shoulders and George
loved it. I came along to interpret if necessary. The Bishop's
two guards were left behind with the other archers at our new
camp. They were told to tend to Brian and Athol, and let no
one near the wagon.

Captain William brought those particular archers, as he explained to me later, because they carried swords in addition to their longbows and knew how to use them.

Our escort of archers waited on shore while a ferryman rowed the four of us out to a relatively large, single-masted, trading cog anchored just off the old stone quay. Its leather sail was furled and it looked deserted. It looked old and derelict.

Young George held tightly to his father's hand as the little dinghy swayed each time the ferryman's oars dug into the water. Then the ferryman hailed the cog and we climbed up and over its deck railing without waiting for a response—with Thomas going first so William could hand George up to him.

As we came aboard, I heard Captain William point out the cog's two little castles at the front and rear of its deck and tell him it was much like the two cogs which had carried him and his Uncle Thomas and the other archers to the Holy Land from England.

"That's when King Richard brought us out to join him in his crusade," Captain William explained.

Ah. That's who they are; crusaders trying to go home.

****** *Yoram*

A ferret-faced little seaman with long scraggly hair met us at the railing as we climbed aboard. He obviously recognised me from my two earlier visits on behalf of the bishop; for without saying a word he pointed to the smaller of the two castles, the one at the front of the cog.

As we walked down the dirty wooden deck we could see into the narrow entrance of the unlit little castle at the front of the cog. A sailor with a bushy beard and his hair in a tarry pigtail was spooning something into a man's mouth from a wooden bowl. A couple of similarly pigtailed sailors were lounging in the sun next to the castle door in an effort to get warm.

Other than the men we could see, the cog seemed damp and unloved and deserted. None of the crew appeared to be concerned about the weapons we were carrying; if they were, they didn't show it.

"This is my lord, Captain William," I announced in the local dialect as we approached the castle door. The two sailors sitting against the wall stood up and moved towards us to listen.

"He and the priest are here to see the Captain."

The Captain's little castle at the front of the cog was absolutely foul and barely large enough for two or three people to be in it at the same time. So Father Thomas stayed on the deck by the door with George while Captain William and I ducked our heads and entered. *It smelt horrible.*

The poor wretch we'd come to see looked to be in terrible shape even though he was able to talk, and smelled worse what with all the shite he was lying in.

I'd never seen anyone looking so dreamy-eyed and lost and devastated all at the same time. They say it's the night air and the bad wine the brothel girls drink what causes his kind of pox.

"Go away unless you've got herbs and medicines to cure me," the poor man mumbled when his eyes focused enough to see us.

Captain William answered him, rather sprightly.

"Well, I just might have what you want. I've got gold coins you can use to buy them and I want to buy your boat."

"Which boat? I've got three."

I was surprised when Captain William's eyes lit up at the answer.

"Three?" Captain William asked with a question in his voice. "Tell me about them."

"See for yourself. I've got the two galleys tied alongside and this here trading cog I took off an ugly Frenchman south of Sicily last year. Forty-four oars to a side, my galleys are. Fast war galleys, and Moorish made with two banks of oars each; but they're not for sale."

The poxed captain spoke slowly as if he was having trouble getting the words out.

My new lord was lost in thought. But only for a moment.

"If you had gold bezants, you could go ashore and get cured, and then buy more galleys and cogs."

What followed was rather interesting. The Captain's eyes lost a bit of their glassy look as he tried again to focus them— and my new lord told the Captain he had fifty gold coins from Constantinople, real bezants, he'd be willing to risk if the cog and galleys were in good enough shape.

The poxed captain laughed rather strangely as if he was drunk, and responded to my new lord's offer by saying he'd stay aboard and die before he'd even think about selling one of his boats for such a low price.

But then the poor wretch confounded me by suggesting eight hundred, or probably even more than nine hundred, gold bezants would be a fair price for good boats like his, if he wanted to sell, which he didn't.

My new lord laughed in return. He replied he'd need to inspect the boats to make sure they were made of silver and precious stones before he could agree to anything close to such an outrageously high price.

So after a lot more talk, that's exactly what we did; we inspected the captain's boats. The ferret-faced sailor came with us as we looked them over. And, at Father Thomas's insistence, young George came with us too. Captain William started to disagree but Father Thomas cut him off with a curt comment.

"He needs to know about such things and see them for himself."

******

Boats like the poxed captain's are called cogs. They have one or two square sails and a cargo hold below their decks and two tiny little castles—one at each end of the top deck—one for the captain in the front and a somewhat larger one in the back for the sailors who work the cog's sails and the rudder oars they row to steer it.

The hold of the cog we were inspecting was empty and smelly with a couple of feet of filthy water sloshing about as it gently rolled from side to side, as the wind and the waves in the harbour rocked it.

The ferret-faced sailor showing us around mumbled something about it being time to bail out the hold again even though the cog "don't leak as much as some I've been on."

In slightly better shape were the poxed Captain's two galleys. Perhaps it was because they had slaves who could be unchained one at a time and made to throw their shite over the side, or bail out the water and piss when it got too high.

When we visited the first galley, we found its slaves hunched in the dank and chilly space under the upper rowing deck and chained to their positions on the rowing benches for the lower bank of oars.

It was the first time I'd ever been on a war galley, and it smelled even worse down there with the slaves than in the captain's castle, and that's saying something, what with all the shite on the captain and all over his bed. Obviously, no one had been unchained and allowed to clean up around the slaves for a long time.

Other than being so foul, it was a normal war galley. Its rowers, usually slaves for the lower of the two banks of oars, sat under the galley's low decks on rowing benches, two men to an oar. And that's where they were when we visited them. It was where they ate, shite, and rowed until they died.

The upper bank of oars was where the galley's sailors and fighting men sometimes sat and rowed to give a galley extra speed until the fighting began.

We climbed down the three wooden steps and bent our heads to walk into the slaves' foul chamber. There wasn't much room between the rowing benches and the deck overhead.

The bent-over slaves raised their heads as much as they could when we walked in. They said not a word but they certainly looked at us intently as the scraggly, greasy-haired seaman explained what we already knew—during a chase, the slaves stayed there while the sailor men and soldiers sat at the upper bank of oars and helped row until they could grapple their victim and climb aboard.

Captain William seemed quite interested in the slaves.

"Are any of you from King Richard's lands?" Captain William thundered in English in a loud and commanding voice and then in French. "England or Wales or France?"

Little George was wide-eyed and holding his nose; that's how I felt, but I was trying to copy Captain William and not show it.

Four or five men sitting together on the left quickly raised their hands and began talking and shouting to us all at the same time. They were, we soon discovered, what was left of a crew of English sailors taken last summer when their Southampton cog was captured.

Our talking to them set off the other slaves and they all began clamouring in various foreign tongues. Two or three seemed to be trying to talk to us in some sort of French, but there was such a clamour and babble of strange tongues I couldn't tell one from another.

"Is this galley sound and seaworthy?" Captain William shouted over the din of the shouting and gesturing slaves.

"Aye, Your Lordship, it is. And it could be made much better as well."

That was the loud response in English from a pock-faced man with a scar along the side of his face and scraggly, long, red hair hanging almost to his waist.

Captain William nodded thoughtfully at him. Then he turned and looked at Father Thomas. Father Thomas nodded back and something seemed to pass between them.

Then we went back up on deck and climbed over the railing to get onto the other galley, the one tied alongside of the galley we were on. It was in much the same shape as the first galley we looked at except that it had no English-speaking slaves. Then the sailors helped us climb back up on to the cog's deck again.

****** *Yoram*

An hour and much shouting and hand waving later, my new lord and the poxed captain spat on the palms of their hands and shook on a price of three hundred and eighty bezant gold coins for the three boats and all their slaves and stores. It was, I thought, far too much; but I didn't say anything. It was, however, quite clear that Captain William needs me.

"Yoram, please go ashore and tell the archers to come to the quay immediately and bring all of our people and goods," he said.

"Tell them to bring everything at the same time, mind you. Don't let them leave the chests unguarded for even a moment. We'll bring the cog and galleys to the quay and moor them there while we load our wounded men and the chests. That way we won't have to risk carrying them in a dinghy and dropping them into the water.

"After you bring the archers to the quay and unload the chests and the two wounded archers, I want you to take Raymond with you and sell the horses and the wagon and the camel in the livestock market. Raymond knows horses, so let him sell them for whatever he can get.

"Use the coins they fetch to buy a jug of good olive oil and two amphora of corn for each boat and firewood so we can make flatbread whilst we're at sea. Also, buy some long hooded rain skins for George and the rest of us to sleep under in case it gets cold on the water."

Then Captain William called after me as I turned to go.

"Oh, Yoram, and please fetch a couple of big cheese wheels for each boat if you can find them and a couple of dozen laying hens."

Later, I learnt that Father Thomas insisted we should feed cheese, eggs, and meat to George every day. I don't know why;

my brothers and I grew up fine on bread and porridge until the coughing pox took them. But what a boy should eat is not worth arguing about; besides, maybe the Greek who told Father Thomas to let boys eat all they want was right. It can't hurt, can it?

Lord William smiled and nodded his agreement when I suggested I should wait on the quay until all three of his new boats are moored to it to make sure the chests were always guarded. "Yes, Lord William, I will wait on the quay.

And then Lord William truly surprised me.

"Yoram, I'm the captain of the company and my Christian name is William. I'm not a lord and I have no family name. I'm just "William" or "Captain" and that is how you should name me. Either is acceptable. It's the proper thing to do since I am the captain and William is only name I've ever had since I was birthed. So please don't name me as "Lord" when you speak to me. Do you understand?"

"Yes, Lord William, I understand. Thank you." *And from the look he gave me, I knew I should have said "Yes, Captain."*

****** *Yoram*

Our new boats soon arrived and were tied up at the city's stone quay. Then Captain William gave me two gold bezants from his purse for the food. Then he smiled and nodded again and gave me two more when I suggested I might need more coins to buy so much.

I also suggested I should buy the food and use the wagon to bring it to the boats before I sold it and the wagon horse.

"Good thinking," William told me with a big smile. And then he once again truly surprised me.

"While you and Raymond are off to the market to do all that I am going to free the slaves and offer them an opportunity to stay with us."

"You aren't going to sell them, Captain William?"

"No. My brother convinced me long ago that no man should be a serf or slave; and if he makes his mark and joins us, he'll have a position with the company so long as he obeys my orders and honours his liege."

Liegemen like me should be rewarded, of course. But slaves and serfs?

"Of course, liege men like me and contract men should be free except for the obligations we accept, My Lord. But slaves and serfs?"

Captain William was emphatic.

"There will be no slaves and serfs on our boats and lands. Not now; not ever."

It was not until much later that I learnt William and Thomas had been birthed as serfs and had somehow escaped when Thomas caught an abbot's eye and was taken off to live in a monastery. Until then, I didn't understand their feelings.

Once again, I turned to go and once again William called me back.

"Wait, there's something else—when you and Randolph and Raymond go to the market I want you to casually walk by the church and look to see if it still seems to be locked up with the bodies in it.

"If the church is still locked up, tell the merchants and the people camping around it that the Bishop is down with the little pox and the church can't be used until it is smoked by special incense from Jerusalem and enough prayers are said by the priests in Beirut.

"If the merchants ask, which they certainly will, tell them that you are helping the sick captain buy food for his boats as part of the payment for the boats to carry the Bishop to Rome when he recovers from his pox."

Chapter Three

Yoram the scribe

My purchases were already being unloaded on to the quay from the wagon by the cog's sailors when the archers gathered in a little group around my new lord and the priest named Thomas, who I now knew for sure to be his brother. It was mid-afternoon and the wind had picked up a bit.

The archers looked intense and concerned and chilled by the wind as William stood on the damp stones of the quay to speak to us. A very worried Brian looked on from his place on the litter that was left behind when the camel was sold. Athol sitting next to him just looked off into the sky with a vacant stare.

"Alright, my friends, here is what we are going to do. I just bought those three boats behind me to carry us back to England. And right . . ."

Before William could continue there was a great shouting and cheering and the men all surged forward to shake his hand and pat him on the back. Several of them looked to be near to tears in their excitement.

After a while, William raised his hands to quiet the men and continued.

"And right here, before we sail for England, every one of us is going to be paid the four gold coins each of us has earned."

There were a lot more cheers and shouts. People walking and working on the quay and the nearby rocky beach heard the noise and were looking at us.

"As you know," William said with a twinkle in his eye and voice, "Thomas and I used our four coins, and some additional bezants we found, to buy these boats and the food we'll need to get us home to England." *Thomas? Not Father Thomas? My new lord is a very strange man.*

The men all laughed and smiled when William said they'd "found" the bezants—the two Bobs and Raymond must have spread the word about the Bishop and what was in the chests.

"We'll use the rest of the coins to hire men to help us row and fight off any pirates who might come our way, and to pay a barber to cut the arrow out of Brian's leg and bleed Athol all right and properlike.

"But there is more—on the way home to England I intend for the company to use the boats to earn more coins by carrying refugees and their goods to safety from the Saracens."

Then William took a deep breath and continued.

"So here's the thing—every archer who makes his mark on a new contract to stay with the company for two more years will not only receive his four gold coins before we sail from here to England, he'll also receive his food and three more gold bezants at the end of each additional year and be a sergeant over the new men we are going to recruit to fill our ranks.

"So it's four gold bezants before we sail no matter what each man decides to do, and three more each year thereafter for every man who stays with us and is willing to serve as a sergeant over the new men we are going to recruit.

"That is enough gold coins, my dear friends, for every man here, including Brian and Athol, to buy his own land and build his own house." The men cheered again. Particularly Brian, the poor bugger. Athol just looked around without seeing anything.

William nodded to his brother.

"Today is the day for the first of everyone's gold coins, right here and right now," shouted the whiskered priest with the ragged robe.

"Everyone line up to get his first gold coin—and a real gold bezant from Constantinople is what it will be. Rain or shine, tomorrow morning, right here on this quay, when the sun begins to pass overhead, every man will get his next three. We'll be sailing three hours after the sun begins travelling up over the horizon to warm us."

When Father Thomas finished, my new lord spoke up again.

"We'll be needing more men for you all to be sergeants over and to help row us home. So while you're in the taverns and whorehouses tonight, I want you to pass the word that in the morning, right after you receive your next three gold bezants, Father Thomas and I will talk to any sailor or fighting man about making his mark to join our company.

"Let it be known that every man who makes his mark on our company roll will get his food and drink and one gold bezant at the end of each year he serves. Each of you, every man who walked here with me and Father Thomas, and Yoram as well, will get three bezants each year and be their sergeants."

Then William bent over and spoke quietly with Brian while Father Thomas and I stood and watched as a dozen or so of the cheerful and excited and newly rich archers rushed off to the city's alehouses and whorehouses to begin spending their riches and celebrating their promotions.

Within minutes, only three of the archers and my new lord and his son and the priest remained on the stone quay along with the two injured men on the camel litter and the two newly recruited Bishop's guards.

"Will they come back, Lord William?" I asked. *I am not comfortable using just William.*

"Oh, I should think so. Who'd want to stay here and wait for the Saracens when they can go to England and be rich?—and, as you know I am well short of being a lord; please just call me William or Captain."

******

There was a surprise waiting for us the next morning when the sun appeared on its daily journey around the world, a big surprise. The old stone quay in front of our three boats was covered with people and more were coming. Most of them were men but there were a number of women and children among them.

We watched them arrive as we stood on the cog's deck and ate a proper breakfast of the bread and cheese I bought yesterday in the local market. There was even a duck egg, which Father Thomas broke open and poured on little George's bread.

Our two galleys were both tied to the stone quay. Our cog with the coin chests, however, had been anchored a few paces off of it for safety's sake.

When we finished breakfast, three of the cog's sailors rowed a line ashore in the cog's dinghy. Then they tied it to the quay and used it to pull in the cog and moor it to the quay.

As soon as the cog was properly secured, we all climbed down to the quay including little George. *They seem to take him everywhere. I wonder why?*

All the archers who didn't spend the night with us on the cog were waiting together in a little group on the quay. They'd helped the sailors pull in the cog and then walked over to us as we began climbing off it.

Most of the archers looked terrible after their night of drinking, and some of them were obviously still drunk. But their eyes got bright and satisfied smiles quickly appeared on all their faces when they reached William and he immediately began handing them their promised coins.

That's when we got a bit of a shock.

Pandemonium broke out when the crowd saw the archers walk to meet us, and it increased when William began handing them their gold bezants. People began to jostle each other and crowd around us shouting and waving and imploring us in a number of tongues.

Everything became clear in a moment—the people gathering around us on the quay and the land behind it desperately wanted to leave with us when we sailed.

Some of the men in the crowd looked familiar. Of course, they were the slaves who went ashore as soon as they were freed. I recognised one of them immediately. He was the redheaded slave with the scar on his face, the one who had been a ship's captain and told us the galley was sound. I think he said his name was Harold.

No wonder I didn't recognise him at first—his hair is cut and he looks cleaner. I wonder how he did it.

******

William took it all in as he handed the archers their coins. Then he gave his son a big hug and kept his arm around him to hold him to his side as he leaned over and quietly gave me new instructions.

"When we finish here, I want you to go to the market and buy more food," he told me. "Get enough to feed one hundred people on each of our three boats for five days. Be sure to fetch a lot more of those big cheeses and all the additional healthy-looking hens you can find for eggs and meat, and enough sacks or amphoras of ground corn for each of the galleys and the cog; get more firewood as well.

"Also, see if you can find a long, hooded robe or jerkin to keep George warm under his rain skin, preferably made of skins instead of cloth, to keep him dry. And I don't think the rain skins you bought yesterday are going to be enough for all our men. Buy one hundred and twenty more of them if you can get them for a reasonable price."

Apparently, it can get cold and wet on the ocean even in the spring. How would I know; I've never been on an ocean, have I?

William gave me five gold bezants and four silver coins from his purse to buy the food and clothes—and once again cautioned me not to pay the merchants a single penny until they "actually deliver everything to us here on the quay." *Of course I wouldn't pay a merchant before he delivered the goods; I'm not a fool, am I?*

"And don't you dare buy any wine. Not one drop. Oh, and buy some more firewood too, short and thin sticks so we can cook on the boats, and some additional water skins or water barrels, if you can find any."

Then he turned towards the rapidly growing crowd around us and raised his hands for silence.

****** *Yoram*

The smiling and newly rich and promoted archer sergeants quickly sobered up and organised the crowd into two lines at William's direction: one for all the people from King Richard's lands and anyone seeking employment on our galleys and cog either as a fighting man or sailor; the other for people willing to pay to be taken to Cyprus.

Everyone else was sent away, and there was much sobbing and crying out from those without coins or jewels. Many of them stayed on the quay and the ground behind it in hopes of a miracle, and several of the women stood in the line to buy passage and offered themselves and their daughters instead of coins.

William selected a number of fighting men and sailors to join us. They included Harold and his fellow English slaves, three men who claimed to be archers and had their own bows, and quite a large number of others who claimed to be sailors or fighting men.

While William spoke with the men who claimed to be soldiers and sailors, Father Thomas and I spoke with those who wanted to buy a passage to Cyprus and collected coins from those who were willing to pay the most.

The people on the quay with us were all quite desperate to leave and Father Thomas and I collected a surprisingly large amount of coins. I know because I helped him talk to the people and counted the coins after we sailed. We got some jewels as well.

We accepted as many of the refugees as we thought we could jam into the three boats. The coins and jewels they paid to go with us almost filled the smelly leather sack Father Thomas found floating in the water in the cog's hold.

And it wasn't just coins the passengers had to provide; every man and woman who paid for a passage also had to agree to take a turn at the oars and wooden bailing buckets if they were needed.

And, of course, those who paid the most wouldn't have to row. They would be carried in the cog which only moved under sail. More importantly, it has two castles on its deck and the deck of the cog covered its hold to keep out the wind and rain.

******

There were more fighting men available than we could possibly carry, including several French knights and a German baron with an entire company of knights and men-at-arms.

We didn't take the baron or any of the knights, even though they had the required coins and many of them were willing to make their marks and join our company; William said they looked too arrogant and dangerous.

Sailors, the English galley slaves, the archers, and an old Jew who claimed to be a barber were the only non-fighting men we took without payment. The Jew agreed pay for his passage by cutting the arrow out of Brian and bleeding poor Athol until he recovered.

The wind had changed by the time we finished loading all the passengers and supplies. As a result, we had to wait until later in the day when the winds became strong enough for the cog to leave.

We were overloaded with passengers and new recruits when we sailed. They were jammed on to the galleys' decks and in the cog's newly bailed out cargo hold, all of which quickly became foul and nasty from our seasick men and passengers even before the wind took us out of the harbour. I got seasick right along with them, and so did William and young George.

When we finally did leave the harbour, we left rich—we had the Bishop's coins and we were loaded with paying passengers.

And, of course, we didn't have any wine to sell to the sufferers of seasickness so they could rinse out their mouths. As it turns out, I could have used some myself and so could everyone else.

******

Our voyage to Cyprus took more than three days. Our two galleys could have made it in half that time using their oars but the cog didn't have the wind it needed and the galleys dared not leave it on its own in these waters and row for Cyprus ahead of it. These waters, if the sailors we recruited were to be believed, were filled with Saracen pirates.

We weren't taking any chances. Captain William was in one of the galleys with young George, me, and half of the coins. Father Thomas was on the other galley with the other half.

The two Bobs and the three archers who did not go to the taverns were in the cog with Randolph as its sergeant. Raymond was with him as his second.

One of the former slaves we'd bought and freed, the English sailor with the scar and the long red hair whose name was Harold, the one who had said he came from someplace in England called Lewes, was appointed by William to be the sergeant of the cog's sailors.

William made Harold up to a sergeant, he told me, because he was an Englishman with lots of experience captaining and piloting big sailing cogs such as ours. Well, that's what he said he had done; we'd know soon enough if it wasn't true.

The refugees who paid the most coins were in both the cog's fore and aft castles. The rest were crammed into the galleys or were crying and moaning in the cog's cold and damp hold.

******

We made good time the first night but the wind failed in the morning. Then we just drifted and bobbed up and down all day long while just about everyone got seasick including me and my new lord.

I know William got seasick, because I could see him periodically hanging over the rail of our galley like me and everyone else.

No one wanted to eat; obviously, I had bought much too much food. What I should have bought were ropes, which the galleys could have used to tow us and even more skins and carpets to keep us warm. It was spring. Who would have thought it could be so cold out there on the water?

On the second day, the wind picked up and we made good time towards the northwest where Cyprus lies. That's when our barber gave Brian some of the old captain's flower paste to eat and then cut into his leg to dig out the arrowhead. Some of the passengers and I sat on Brian to hold him down while the barber kept cutting deeper and deeper in an effort to get his fingers around the arrowhead so he could pull it out.

Poor Brian screamed and jerked about at first and then suddenly just relaxed and went to sleep for ten or fifteen minutes while the barber hurried to finish his digging.

Chapter Four

Sergeant Yoram

We were going along at a decent clip with each galley's square sails catching the wind and small bursts of periodic rowing to keep up with the cog, when one of our new sailors shouted something out about seeing a sail in the distance.

It was a war galley, a two decker like ours, and it was coming straight at us.

William quickly sent our galley's fighting men to their battle positions and some of our more able-bodied passengers took the places of the fighting men who had been on the rowing benches at the time.

Strangely enough, William decided to wait before he had me take George into the captain's little castle in the front of the galley—because, as told me later, he wanted George to see what fighting men do to get ready before the fighting starts.

He wanted the boy to see how we get ready? Why would he do that?

Father Thomas and William looked at each other across the water between their galleys. I watched as they nodded to each other in agreement.

I knew their plan. I'd been in the cog's forward castle with them before we sailed and listened when they and Randolph and Harold, the red-haired former slave, discussed the possibility we'd encounter pirates and agreed on what our galleys would do if it happened.

If there is more than one pirate galley, they intend to have our galleys lie near the cog on either side of it and wait for the pirates to come to us.

On the other hand, if there was only one pirate galley, they would wait until it almost reached us and then leave the cog and go straight at it—and throw our anchors on its deck to grapple its hull on both sides while our archers raked its crew with their arrows.

Either way they would keep our archers out of sight until the last minute and not stray far from the cog and leave it unprotected.

The plan did not work.

Everyone got ready and we waited anxiously—but the unknown galley suddenly veered off and soon disappeared over the horizon to the front and left of us, the direction our sailors call "port" even when there isn't one in sight. It turned away and was gone before our two galleys had a chance to pull away from the cog and row towards it.

The only interesting thing is we didn't know anything about the galley; it flew no flag—but then we weren't flying any flags either.

Later, we talked it over and decided our sailors were right—someone up on the enemy galley's mast must have seen our archers crouching below the railings on the sides of our galleys' hulls.

Harold, the man Captain William appointed sergeant of the cog's sailors because he'd been a cog's master before being taken as a slave, yelled across the water to William. He said the pirate galley looked just like the Algerian galley that had taken his cog and sold him into slavery in Tangiers some two years before.

"If it is the same galley," Harold shouted, "it is ever so slightly smaller than ours, with two banks of twenty oars on each side pulled by one slave at each oar in the lower bank of oars and about forty fighting men on board armed with swords. The fighting men," he said, "row from the upper rowing benches until the fighting starts."

The pirates' method for taking a prize, I had heard Harold explain to William and Thomas before we sailed, at least as it had been applied to the taking of his ship two years ago, was to rapidly come along side, grapple its victim, and then swarm aboard with swords and spears—they were all boarders without archers and armour, although, they sometimes carried small shields.

William and Thomas had listened carefully and asked many questions; they obviously considered Harold's observations to be of great value. *I must remember that.*

****** *William*

Cyprus came into view about noon of our third day at sea. I was napping with my son in the little castle at the front of the galley when Yoram came running to tell me land had been sighted and that the sailors said they were sure it was Cyprus.

We turned to the right and rowed along the coast for a while. Four or five hours later, we entered the harbour at Limassol. It was filled with all kinds of boats—including what looked like the Algerian galley we'd seen earlier, as well as a number of large, single-masted trading cogs like ours.

There were also quite a few little fishing boats either in the water or beached on the strand. I could see the logs the fishermen use as rollers to help pull their boats up on to the strand and get them back out into the water. I'd seen the same thing in Latika while I was waiting for the Bishop to make up his mind about leaving.

We were more than a little surprised to see the Algerian galley because Cyprus has been under Christian rule for several centuries. It was a Roman Catholic kingdom and has been for several years, ever since King Richard captured it from its governor—who answered to the Orthodox Christian Church in Constantinople—and then promptly sold it to the Order of Templars, who then got rid of the Orthodox churchmen and just as quickly sold it to Guy de Lusignon, who just as promptly proclaimed the Kingdom of Cyprus with him as king.

It had all been arranged.

It was all quite confusing, but now, at least so far as we knew, Cyprus was still a Christian kingdom except that it had a Roman Catholic king answering to the Pope in Rome in order to maintain his divine rights to his kingship, instead of an Orthodox king answering to the Patriarch in Constantinople.

Either way, Cyprus was relatively safe for Christians. That's probably why so many of the refugees trying to escape from the Saracens wanted to come there. It certainly was why we were making Cyprus our first stop on our way back to England.

We archers knew all about Cyprus becoming Roman Catholic. We'd briefly fought here to help Richard take it some years ago in order to rescue his future queen. She and Richard's sister were taken for ransom by Cyprus' Orthodox governor when the women's ship got separated from Richard's in a storm and fetched up here.

Indeed, we were with Richard right here in Limassol when he married Queen Berengaria—and then went crusading with him on a good contract until it expired right after he slaughtered the Saracens we had captured at Acre. It's a good thing we didn't renew it—he abandoned his crusade to return to England without taking his men home, even though providing for their return was in their contracts.

Unfortunately, or perhaps fortunately as it turned out, we stayed in the Holy Land and took up a contract with Lord Edmund to fight against the Saracens who had begun advancing on the crusader lands. It was probably fortunate we stayed, since the rumours at the time had Richard and everyone travelling with him missing and believed to be either dead or taken as slaves or being held for ransom. The rumours turned out to be true.

In any event, we reached Cyprus with our seasick crew and passengers, and everyone else, including our archers and me and my son, desperately anxious to get off the boats and plant our feet on dry land. And that's exactly what happened—there was a mad stampede to get off our boats as soon as we tied up at the quay in front of the Limassol city walls.

I allowed our sailors and fighting men to get off when the passengers did. I could hardly do otherwise since I desperately wanted to get off myself. But it had been years since we were last here and I wasn't going to take any chances—I ordered all of our men to arm themselves and stay on either their boat or on the quay. I wanted them nearby in case we need to fight the Algerians or make a hasty departure.

Most of the men grudgingly complied, but several ran and more than a few of the new men slipped off to the city's ale houses and taverns after the sun finished passing overhead and darkness fell that night.

And, of course, Thomas and I were immediately accosted by a port official who wanted a mooring fee for the use of the quay. He accepted a gold bezant for all three boats and quickly disappeared. An hour later, we learnt the mooring fee was much less and must be paid at the harbourmaster's office inside the city gate nearest the harbour. We'd been gulled.

****** *William*

One of the passengers on the cog was a tough-looking Jewish merchant. He got off and walked away with the other merchants we were carrying as soon as the cog was tied up to the city's quay. But then he returned about thirty minutes later to speak with me just as the false port official was leaving.

Yoram brought the merchant to me on the quay and stood by in case I needed a translator. I didn't, of course, because, like most of the merchants in the ports hereabouts, the man was multi-lingual and could gobble both Latin and the bastardised Norman French of the English Crusaders some are now calling English.

Our visitor was a merchant, one of the paying passengers we carried with us from Latika in the cog's stern castle. He wanted to know if we intend to return to Syria to get more passengers and their coins. If we do, he told me, he wanted to buy a passage and return with us.

The man's name was Reuben something or other and he said he was from Latika, the port city from which we'd sailed. He'd also asked me the day before whether we planned to return and pick up another load of refugees, but I'd been too seasick to pay him much mind at the time.

"You want to return? But then why did you come?"

"To carry coins and arrange for the shipment of the things my father and his friends want me to buy for them in Cyprus."

"I'll carry you back with a place in the cog's rear deck castle and your bread and cheese for two gold bezants or their equivalent," I told him. He'd paid five to travel here, but I knew we'd otherwise be going back empty so two seemed fair.

"But I have no idea when that will be—we are not going back for more refugees until we find a defensible house or an extremely safe place to camp. We need some kind of safe place where we can care for our wounded men and protect my son and our possessions."

I was emphatic.

"Until we find such a place, we are going to stay on our boats where it is safer for us."

Reuben smiled at me and nodded his head.

"Perhaps I can help you find what you want. I have relatives and fellow merchants who have spent their entire lives here on Cyprus."

******

My men and I spent a damp and restless spring night shivering on the cog with our galleys tied along its sides for protection.

In the middle of the night, one of our lookouts gave us quite a start. He suddenly shouted a warning that the Algerian galley, for that's what it was according to the men who visited the taverns and whorehouses last night, was getting underway on the other side of the harbour.

Everyone stood to arms immediately and listened to the swish and splashes of its oars as the Algerian moved past us and headed towards the harbour entrance.

We were concerned, of course, that the Algerians might be launching a surprise attack to cut out one or all of our boats. But we need not have worried—it went right on by us. We watched in the moonlight until it disappeared out of the harbour and passed into the darkness.

In a way, it was a pity the Algerians decided to leave—because Thomas and I had been thinking about using our newly recruited men to launch a cutting out expedition of our own. We had in mind to take the Algerian galley for ourselves and add it to our little fleet. But in the end, we decided not to try because we have other plans for Cyprus and we weren't sure how the authorities here in Limassol might react if we started a battle right here in the harbour—*if there are any authorities here now that King Guy's court is elsewhere on Cyprus.*

Finally, Thomas and I talked it over and decided it was just as likely our men who slipped away to the taverns last night alerted the Algerians to our strength—and they left because they were concerned that we might try to take their galley instead of the other way around.

******

Early the next day as the sun came up there was a loud hail from the nearby shore. Reuben the Jewish merchant was back—and he'd brought a couple of men and a horse-drawn wagon with him. There were also a number of men standing around on the quay waiting for us to come ashore.

"There is a place you might find interesting," Reuben shouted out to me from the beach as I leaned over the rail and cupped my hand to my ear to better hear him.

"It's right outside the city walls. It's a good location because it means you can come and go as you please."

I looked at Thomas, and Thomas raised his eyes and gave me a little "why not" shrug of his shoulders.

"All right. We'll look at it. Give us a couple of minutes."

Before I left, I ordered Randolph and the two Bobs to stay on board our boats with most of the archers to guard them.

And, of course, in so doing, guard George and the coins, though we were careful to never talk about the coins at all, not even to our veteran archers—because we wanted everyone to think they'd all been used to pay the men and buy the boats and food.

****** *Yoram the Scribe*

A few minutes after Reuben hailed us from the shore, my new lord emptied the galleys of everyone except Brian and Athol and a couple of sailors to tend them. Then he told about thirty of our fighting men to prepare to come ashore to accompany him and Father Thomas to wherever it was the merchants wanted to take us. And, once again, young George came with us.

All the rest of our archers and other fighting men were sent to the cog and told to stay there to defend our boats until we returned. Randolph was to be in command as the master sergeant over them all until we return. And, of course, as I heard William explain to Father Thomas, Randolph was to lead a rescue force if things went badly on this unknown shore.

I went ashore with William and Thomas to translate if a translator was needed—and was pleased to be included. The rest of the men were told to practice with their weapons and stay on board the galleys. Our galleys were securely lashed to either side of the cog which was now anchored in the middle of the harbour.

Each of the Bobs, Long Bob from Chester and Bob who'd been a serf on a corn farm in York until he went for an archer, was made the sergeant captain of one of the galleys, and

Randolph made the master sergeant over them and was given charge of the cog and the overall command of the three boats.

William and Thomas obviously thought they were among the most dependable of their men.

And, yes, I definitely approved of the way William was taking no chances. This effort to get him ashore might be a ruse to take our boats. The Algerian galley may have gone out in the night but it could be somewhere nearby and up to no good.

William and Father Thomas and I studied the waiting merchants and the gathering crowd as one of the seamen rowed us to shore in the cog's dinghy. They didn't look dangerous.

At the same time, in response to some orders my new lord shouted out as we climbed down to the dinghy, one of the galleys was untied from the cog and began rowing its way to the quay to unload the men who would go with us to be our guards. It was to wait for us there until we returned.

Not one of the three merchants was armed, so perhaps taking so many men as our guards was not necessary. On the other hand, neither William nor Thomas had been here for some years; Cyprus and its dangers were no longer known to them.

"Greetings and a good day to you, Master Merchant, and what is it that you have to show us?"

That was Father Thomas's cheerful greeting to Reuben and the other man waiting with him as Captain William, Father Thomas, and I jumped one at a time from the front of the dinghy and on to the beach next to the quay.

"There is an old, fortified stone farm house that might suit you for your quarters," Reuben replied in English. The other merchant nodded his agreement to show us that he too knew how to gobble it.

"It's outside the city walls," Reuben went on to explain, "and not in the best of condition—but you can see the boats in the harbour from it and it could be quickly repaired. Indeed, it could be turned into a rather safe and secure little citadel if you have the men to do the work or are willing to hire local men to do it for you."

Before William could answer, we were besieged with cries and entreaties from the men on the beach who had begun gathering around us. They looked and sounded like a bunch of sailors and soldiers seeking employment. And that was exactly what they were. With a few exceptions they were a rather motley-looking crew of destitute men who had somehow made their way here.

"I am interested," William assured Reuben as he held up his hand to stop him from continuing. "But first I must deal with these men.

"And give our archers and other fighting men who are still unloading from the galley time to get here before we go off with him," he said to me very quietly out of the side of his mouth.

Then William turned and shouted to the gathering crowd in English and then again in French. He pointed at Father Thomas as he spoke.

"Are there any men who speak English or want to join our company as archers, fighting men, or sailors? If so, get in line and speak to the priest."

Men jostled each other and hot words were exchanged in a number of tongues as Father Thomas and I got the waiting people in a semblance of a line to be interviewed. They all wanted employment except for some who wanted to buy passages to other places. A few even wanted to buy passages back to the Holy Land.

This time, at least, there were no desperate women offering themselves and their daughters.

Captain William spoke quietly with the merchants while Father Thomas and I interviewed the men in the various languages they spoke. Within minutes we added about two dozen men to our company.

What was quite interesting, I think, is what Father Thomas told the men who were not selected—he said those of them who were still willing to make their marks to join us would be considered again if we acquire more galleys. *Now why would he say that?*

****** *William*

The arrival of Reuben and his merchant friends was quite timely. Our plan for Cyprus and the immediate future had been pretty much settled the night before when Thomas and I talked on the deck of the cog out of earshot of our men.

Thomas was going to remain in Cyprus with my son, our two wounded men, five or six of our most dependable archers, and some forty or so of the more likely looking of our new men as guards.

I, on the other hand, would take the two galleys and return to Latika, and maybe even Acre, to rescue more paying passengers—but not until we found a defensible place to store our coins and shelter my son and our people.

Unfortunately, we didn't know what we should do with the cog and its cargo. We finally decided to try to sell it in Cyprus.

But, first and foremost, we needed to find a warm and defensible place where Thomas and the men who were sheltering with him could protect George and our chests of coins. I was not about to return to the Holy Land for more coins and refugees until after we had such a place.

****** *William*

We walked with the two merchants on the track along the beach, and George rode on the wagon with the grizzled old man driving the horse. He sat on the bench next to the driver and was quite proud of himself—and watched the horse intently when he was allowed to hold the reins. *He's a good lad, my son is.*

While we walked, we talked. What Thomas and I learnt was quite interesting. Reuben periodically risks his life to carry coins and parchments to Cyprus to arrange business transactions and payments between his father's group of merchants in Latika and the merchants here on Cyprus.

What we heard from the merchants was even more interesting. It would be worth a lot of coins to them and the other Cyprus merchants, Reuben's friend suggested—with Reuben nodding his head in enthusiastic agreement—if they could pay for what they bought by giving us coins in one place such as here in Limassol and sending a parchment enabling someone else to pick up the same amount of coins, less a fee of course, in some other place, such as in Syria, at the port of Latika.

"The pirates will leave your galleys and our parchment coin orders alone," Reuben offered with a smile, "as soon as they learn they are full of fighting men and only carry parchment letters instead of actual coins.

"The Venetian merchants and moneylenders are doing this," he told us with grudging admiration, "but they have some kind of contract among themselves so that they only do it for their fellow Venetians."

****** *William*

The name of Reuben's merchant friend was Aaron, Aaron of Limassol. Like Reuben and his family, Aaron's family dealt in olive oil, corn, and firewood—the makings of bread.

What Aaron and Reuben and their fellow merchants in Limassol and Syria wanted soon became clear. They are looking for men with war galleys who will, for a handsome fee, guard their cargos and accept coins handed to them in one place such as Syria and let someone with the proper parchment collect a similar amount of coins in another place, such as Cyprus or Rome or London.

If there is a way such a thing might be arranged, Aaron and Reuben explained, they and their fellow merchants would never have to risk having their coins and their sons travel on the ocean for the pirates to capture. Having such a service would, they implied, be worth many gold bezants.

It was an interesting idea and Thomas and Yoram were quite taken by it; I could tell by the look on their faces and intense way they listened. It sounded good to me too.

******

Reuben and Aaron were taking us to see an old abandoned stone house just outside the city walls on the south side of

Limassol. They pointed it out to us as we came around the southern end of the city wall.

Once it might have been a fortified farm-house or caravanserai, or perhaps a Roman trading station, or even the small castle of a minor noble or city official. Unfortunately, its best days were obviously many years ago and it had long since been abandoned and fallen into decay.

It was in bad shape. Almost all of its slate roof had collapsed when its wooden roof beams rotted away, and the curtain wall surrounding its bailey had fallen down in several places.

"It was abandoned when the earth shook and killed people in my grandfather's day," volunteered another English-gobbling merchant who had walked up to join the conversation with a cheery wave to Reuben and Aaron.

"Moslem witches caused the shaking when the Orthodox priests came from Constantinople and killed the Moslem priests. At least, that's what the peasants say."

Whatever the cause, the place was totally unusable. The curtain wall enclosing its courtyard, which we in England call a bailey, was not only falling over, it was almost too short to do any good. It was barely high enough to keep horses and cattle in let alone keep robbers and thieves out. Some things were missing altogether. For example, there was no gate in the curtain wall and no door for the entrance into the building.

All in all, it was a right proper mess and there were squatters living in it who jumped up and ran as we approached.

In other words, it would be perfect if we could buy it and fix it up.

"Who owns it?" I inquired.

"It's been like this so long ago that no one remembers." The answer came from yet another of Aaron's merchant friends who had joined our little group while we stood there talking and looking at the place.

At least, I think that's what he said. I couldn't tell for sure because he gobbled his answer in French and his French had a heavy accent.

My French was barely usable. Other than the Latin Thomas taught me to read and scribe, all I can speak is my mother tongue some are now calling English.

"What will the new king do if we improve the place and turn it into something of a fortress?" I asked.

"Not much, I would think," answered Aaron. Then he explained why.

"The King is never here. He only visited once several years ago. Although, to be honest with you, the French knight who recently arrived to act as the King's local governor may try to extort taxes and protection monies from you as he does from all the local merchants and farmers.

"Unfortunately, the Frenchman hasn't been here long enough for us to know how serious his threats are. All we know is that he is some kind of distant relation of the King's and had never been out of France until he arrived here."

Then Aaron and his merchant friends tried to explain the realities of local life in Limassol. It seemed the King's local governor is a tax farmer. He has an amount he must pay the King each year, and for his trouble gets to keep everything else he can collect.

"It's a negotiation," one of the other merchants suggested.

"Because the governor knows if he asks too much we'll move away and he'll get nothing. On the other hand, this new one seems to be pretty stupid so you never know."

"And it doesn't matter what we merchants have to pay—you and your men will pay the governor very little indeed," laughed Aaron. Then he explained why.

"He'll worry that if he asks for more than a token you'll just sail away and leave him without even a small copper coin. But even more important, he'll see you have more archers and soldiers than he has so he'll know you can make him an offer he can't refuse—he can stay in the governor's castle on the hill above the city and keep his head, and you can stay down here near the water and keep your coins."

We all laughed. *But is that really how it would work?*

Chapter Five

Sergeant Yoram

"It will be dangerous at first," I heard Father Thomas warn Captain William after we returned to the boats, "particularly if you go sailing off to get more refugee coins before we have a safe fortress to protect us.

"Word is bound to get out that you and most of our men are gone and the coin chests and George are here with a priest and a few guards. Even the Algerians might come back and try. Or, God forbid, they might come back with more men and heathen galleys to help them."

Captain William agreed, and I found it most pleasant because he mentioned me so favourably when he did.

"Other than Yoram, we can't be sure of the men who made their mark in Latika. A leader may arise from among them who will set them upon us. If we are to do this, you'll have to wave your cross a lot while I am away—and keep the gates closed and the archers alert."

"Aye, you're right, William. Our own archers are the only men we can depend on until we come to know the new men better."

Two hours later, a decision was reached at the end of a meal of bread and cheese washed down with bowls of morning ale from the city. We scooped it from a leather bucket with our wooden bowls and it was quite good on a fairly warm spring day.

I was the only other person who knew what William and Thomas had decided—to sell the cog as soon as possible and use the coins to begin rebuilding the old building. That way no one would know they had other coins with them that could be stolen or robbed. Of course, I told them I agreed with what they had decided; I was honoured to be present and included in the discussion.

They also agreed only to return to Latika and the other Holy Land ports to earn more coins carrying refugees to safety *after* our base here was sufficiently fortified and guarded—so George and the coins would be safe when one or both of them left.

"This building is going to be important," Father Thomas said with a satisfied belch as he finished his bowl of ale. "It will be our fortified home, our citadel, if you will, the place where we can protect George and our coins while our two galleys carry passengers and cargos to and from Cyprus to earn more coins."

"We'll need masons and joiners if we are to fix it up enough to be both liveable and defensible as such a citadel must be," William cautioned his brother and me. "As it stands, it wouldn't stop a shepherd boy looking for his goats."

"We can restack the fallen stones by ourselves and it won't cost us a copper," Thomas replied. "We've the men to do it. But the only joiner in the archers fell so long ago I can't even remember his name, just that he made particularly straight arrow shafts. Arlon, I think it might have been. Perhaps some of the new men know how to work with wood. We'll have to ask them."

And that is exactly what we did—and we found not a single man.

******

William was on the beach at the end of the quay waving his hand in a circle over his head in the archer's signal to come to him as he shouted for everyone to assemble around him. It was an important moment for us all, and I remember it well.

When perhaps half of our company were in a big circle around him, William informed everyone we would be staying here for a while before we returned to England.

He told the men we were going to establish a permanent base on Cyprus; we'd spend the winter here so our galleys could earn more coins rescuing Christians and Jews from the Saracens.

Then, with me interpreting for those who couldn't speak French or English, William asked if any of our men were joiners or boat wrights or masons. Several of the new men raised their hands and came forward. The rest of the men were dismissed to prepare for the move to our new home and to inform the men who were not present of the decision.

There was, no question about it, grumbling from several of the archers who wanted to go to England straightaway.

Later, when he heard about the grumbling, Captain William agreed that those who wished to do so could take their name off the company's contract and make their own way home with a gold bezant to help them on their way—and not a single man accepted.

******

Captain William and Father Thomas spent a few minutes learning the names of the handful of men who come forward and talking to them about their experiences and abilities as craftsmen.

The results were disappointing. Not a one of the men, it seemed, had ever been a journeyman or master and only one claimed to have served as an apprentice joiner. It was a significant disappointment—it meant that if we wanted to fix up the old farmhouse we'd have to find craftsmen in the city or find them among the refugees or bring them in from the Holy Land.

In any event, there was much shouting and moving about after William's announcement. Certain of the men were told to stay on the boats as guards. The rest were told to march with William to set up a camp at the abandoned ruins which was to be our new home on Cyprus.

******

The first thing my new liege lord did after his announcement was to send Raymond and me to the city's livestock market with a small pouch of silver coins. We were told to buy a horse and wagon to carry George, our two wounded men, and our chests and other possessions from the cog to our new quarters.

Raymond is apparently the only archer who knows anything about horses and livestock. I must remember that.

Father Thomas came with us to see the city and find out what else was available in the local market, such as timber and pots and pans for our new home.

Before we left to enter the city, William charged us with letting the merchants know we were looking for joiners and masons and boat wrights to employ either temporarily or to put their marks on our company's contract and join us permanently. It turned out to be a wise decision, and we learnt something important—a city's merchants inevitably know everything and everyone and are almost always willing to be encouraging and helpful in the hope of obtaining future custom and relationships.

I know it sounds strange, but at the time neither I nor my new lords had realised the merchants would be willing to be so helpful. It proved to be true in city after city.

****** *Yoram*

Our visit to the city's market was quite revealing. To my surprise, Reuben and Aaron met us at the edge of the market to show us around and introduce us to the merchants.

I wonder why they are being so helpful and how they knew we were coming?

Limassol was large enough for all kinds of things to be available in its market. And to our surprise, mine at least, much of what the merchants were selling in their shops was manufactured in the work places that lined both sides of its crowded and bustling, cobblestoned market street and the little lanes that ran off it.

The market itself was just outside the city walls, and the local merchants and artisans already seemed to know all about our decision to move into the ruin and repair it.

We received many suggestions and solicitations for our custom as we moved along the market street with Aaron and Reuben pointing out what was available and introducing us to their fellow merchants.

Reuben must come here frequently from Syria. He obviously knows these people.

Then it happened.

There was a clatter of hoofs on the cobblestones and the crowd in the narrow market street scattered as a partially armoured knight and a couple of men-at-arms on horseback trotted up to us with their hands on their sheathed swords. Several people in the crowd called out to warn us that the King's governor was coming as he and his men trotted up to us.

Is he here to intimidate us or to protect us from the merchants and common people who have, according to Reuben, risen several times in the past few years against the king's high taxes?

Reuben and Aaron and I and our escorts instinctively faded back into the crowd. Father Thomas, however, just stood there in the middle of the lane between the stalls and gazed up at the knight on horseback who trotted up to him. He seemed rather serene under the circumstances.

"You there, Priest. Did you come on one of those boats?" The knight said it arrogantly and with menace.

"Yes, I did, Sir Knight. And that's why I know there was an Algerian galley in the port when we arrived. I also know we paid twice for the use of the mooring space on the quay—once to your port sergeant and once to the outlaw who pretended to represent you."

Then Father Thomas stepped towards the knight and spoke even more loudly so all could hear.

"The lord who is the captain of our company found it most curious that the King's governor would allow such behaviour to occur in his city. Why is that? Does the King know you are letting thieves prey on his people so they can't pay his taxes?"

Yes, I now know that William is neither knight nor lord and so, certainly, did Father Thomas. But this man and the people around us did not.

The knight governor was visibly taken aback by Father Thomas's lack of fear and the veiled threat in his response; it was clearly not the response he expected. But he put a great scowl on his face and plunged ahead.

"Watch your tongue, Priest, or you'll find yourself in my dungeon."

Then Father Thomas surprised me and greatly impressed the merchants and everyone else in the city. He walked up to the horse and spoke quietly to the governor. Only the few of us standing nearby could hear what he told him.

"It is much more likely that you'll end up in your king's dungeon than I or any of Lord William's men will end up in yours, Sir Knight," Thomas said softly.

"But what is absolutely certain, Sir Knight, is that you and your men will not live to see the sun finish passing overhead if you make difficulties for us today or any other day. Lord William's men are here in the market in force and there are only three of you—and not enough men in your castle to come to your aid or to defend it if Lord William decides to take your castle from you."

Thomas continued much more loudly, after a pause to allow the surprised knight to absorb what he'd just been told.

"But you are fortunate, Sir Knight, fortunate, indeed— Lord William means you no harm and his presence can only enrich the merchants you tax for your king. Surely, you can see that?"

Father Thomas asked the question with a genial wave of his hand towards the surrounding crowd as he stepped back out of the range of the governor's sword.

It was only then, when the knight instinctively looked towards the crowd and where Father Thomas was gesturing, that his eyes widened—because that's when he first saw the archers of our escort only a few feet away with their longbows fully drawn and their metal tipped arrows pointed straight at his bare face and throat.

At that point, Father Thomas became most conciliatory and began speaking in a normal voice so the merchants standing nearby could also hear.

"Lord William never saves his coins, Sir Knight; he spends them all on the hundreds of veteran fighting men he has brought with him to Limassol to help the refugees trying to flee from the Holy Land to escape the Saracens.

"All of these fine merchants know of his generosity towards his men and the victims of the Saracens, and so does his friend and liege lord King Richard of England who sent him to Cyprus and His Holiness the Pope, who sent me here to advise His Lordship."

It was all pile of ox shite about the King and the Pope, of course, but the governor never knew—at least that's what I thought and Father Thomas confirmed to me later when we walked back to the quay to visit our boats.

With a smile, Father Thomas spread his hands wide and added some honey to his words.

"And now it will be your good fortune to convey to your good king the news of the prosperity and increased tax revenues Lord William's arrival and generosity will bring to him from Limassol. King Guy will be surely pleased."

"Ah, well," answered the pudgy and suddenly sweating governor as he finally realised his danger and slowly pushed his partially drawn sword back down into its sheath, "if that's the case, perhaps all is well, isn't it?"

Then he and his men backed their horses around so they faced the way they'd come and trotted away down the market lane with as much arrogance as they could muster.

Father Thomas and I spent the rest of the afternoon talking to those who were presented to us as the city's master joiners and masons. There were several of each in the city and they all had journeymen and apprentices.

Reuben and Aaron assured us their prices would be reasonable—and implied the merchants would see to it they were because of the importance of keeping us here.

In short order, with the help of the merchants, arrangements were made and all the available master joiners and master masons were told to report for work the next morning with their journeymen and apprentices.

William and Thomas were in a hurry to get the work underway. William wanted to make the farm house defensible as quickly as possible so he could make at least a few coin-earning trips to the Holy Land ports before the coming summer ended and the sea storms arrived.

******

We all slept that night either on the boats or inside the walls of the old ruin under a couple of big tents hastily made from the spare sails Randolph found on the cog. It was a good thing it wasn't raining or particularly cold.

Work began immediately, as soon as the sun came up the next morning. By early afternoon the first of the fallen stones were beginning to be lifted back into place by masons from the city.

It was all quite interesting. The masons and joiners brought strange round contraptions similar to those that sailors use to raise sails; and large timbers and logs soon began arriving and being manhandled into place so they could be trimmed and joined in order to once again hold up the slate roof.

The work was divided among the masters and their men, with the masters providing the expertise and our archers and men-at-arms providing whatever additional help they needed with the lifting and fetching.

When their muscles weren't needed by the craftsman, our fighting men took turns practising with their weapons and using some of the tools we bought in the market to begin digging a moat around the curtain wall enclosing the ruin's little courtyard.

The rocks and stones the moat diggers found would be used to raise the curtain wall and build arrow slits for the archers to shoot through; the dirt would be used to begin the second defensive wall William wants to build out beyond the first one. The new wall would go all the way around the current wall and our little citadel and give us a second and much larger bailey.

At one point I counted almost two hundred men at work. There would have been more except for the eighty or so archers, sailors, and men-at-arms being kept on the boats under the command of one of the most responsible of the archers, Randolph from London.

They were there in case the Algerians returned.

******

Time passed quickly and less than two weeks later, our Cyprus ruin was beginning to take shape and be somewhat defensible.

The slate roof and the wood joining were almost complete; we now had a strong wooden door on the entrance to our little citadel and a strong wooden gate across the entrance to the compound. There were also new wooden plugs that could be pushed into the archer slits to keep the mild chills of the Cyprus winters from coming into the old house.

At least, I least I think winter shouldn't be too bad; yesterday when I was in the market shopping for food, Aaron told me winters here were quite mild, although, sometimes they could be a bit wet.

Last night, for the first time, Captain William, Father Thomas and young George were able to sleep in the loft of our citadel and pull the ladder up after them.

Similarly, the two Bobs and I, and all the rest of the original archers—at least, all those not sleeping on our three boats to guard them—were able to bar the new door and sleep in the hall in front of the little fireplace. The fireplace, of course, was not being used because of the summer heat.

It was a particularly smelly night because of the slop bucket—the stomachs of some of the men, including me, having been turned by bad fish, which somehow found its way into the soup prepared by one of the archers, Thomas the cook.

Most of our men and the new recruits now slept in the bailey outside of our little citadel. Initially, they were sleeping rough or in tents made from old cog sails.

The refugees and freed slaves who were still with us slept as best they could outside our walls. They helped the masons and worked on the walls and in the cook-house in exchange for their food. Some of the more ambitious of them had already built little lean-to shelters for themselves using various materials.

******

"Yoram," Father Thomas called to me when he came down the ladder in the morning.

"Yes, Father Thomas."

"Please go to the cookhouse tent and ask Thomas the cook to bring a big breakfast here for George. Morning ale, Bread, cheese, and at least one chicken or duck egg, and preferably two or three. And bring meat if Thomas Cook has any and it's finished boiling.

"Also, please have someone bring up a bucket of water and a ladle and ask Thomas Cook to bring something for me and William. And have him empty the damn slop bucket, too; we can smell it all the way up here."

Life is getting normal with all the comforts of home. If we stay here much longer, I am going to talk to Captain William about buying some string beds in the market. Sleeping on the stone floor is hurting my hip.

In morning Captain William and Father Thomas announced a decision, and I wasn't at all sure I liked it because

I was certain to be seasick the entire time—Captain William and I would take the two galleys back to Latika on the Syrian coast, and then, perhaps, on to Acre. We would bring back anyone willing to pay for a passage to Cyprus.

Father Thomas would not go with us. He would stay here with young George, six of the English archers, and some of our newly recruited men-at-arms. They'd continue to work with the masons and joiners to improve our new home.

There was still much work to be done to turn the old building into a proper fortress where we could be comfortable and sheltered from our enemies and robbers—we'd barely started work on the second defensive wall and the moat William wanted to run around the whole place to create a much larger outer courtyard. *In England, as I later learnt, a courtyard inside a wall is called a bailey. I wonder why?*

And that wasn't all. According to Captain William, we also needed a barracks inside the bailey where the men could sleep out of the rain, a proper cookhouse for Thomas Cook, and to raise the current curtain wall by installing battlements and archer slits so we could better defend ourselves if we were attacked. And, most of all, we needed to dig a well in the little courtyard so we couldn't be driven out by thirst.

It was quite surprising that we could find no trace of a well. Perhaps that was why the place was abandoned. *Could it be a bad omen?*

Chapter Six

Sergeant Yoram

Father Thomas and little George and some of the men were waving from the Limassol quay as our two galleys rowed out on the morning wind. Both galleys had their short and stubby leather sails up to catch the morning breeze coming off the mountains.

We were sailing for the Holy Land with a full complement of sailors, archers, and men-at-arms at the oars—more than ninety men on each galley including almost all of the experienced archers and men-at-arms we recruited in Cyprus. We had two strong fighting men for every oar. I felt very secure even though I was quite seasick the first day.

Captain William and I were together on one of the galleys with Harold as our pilot and the sergeant of our sailors; Randolph was the sergeant captain of the other galley with a pilot and a sailor sergeant from among the men we recruited in Latika. Some of the men were pleased to be going back for a visit; others were not even though they wouldn't even have to go ashore.

We were also carrying a passenger on our galley—the merchant who had travelled with us from Latika and helped us find our new home and the men and materials to begin repairing it.

The passenger's name was Reuben and I came to know all about him on the voyage. He was a merchant in Latika merchant and we both originally lived in Damascus until our families were forced to leave because of a religious disputes with the Saracebs—he because he because his family wouldn't abandon being Jews; me because mine wouldn't abandon being Christians. We shared a bed with the galley's sergeants in the little deck castle in the stern; William and Harold shared the even smaller castle in the bow.

Reuben's family sells corns and oils, and he'd even heard of the man who taught me to do sums and scribe years ago. It's a small world and we talked about it constantly. It helped make the voyage more bearable.

It was surprisingly chilly on the water, and I promptly got seasick and had to stick my head out of an oar hole and barf; and so did Reuben and William and a many of the men.

The good news, at least I thought it was good news, was that William decided we should row all the way and not use our sails once Cyprus was behind us. He wanted to know how fast we could move between Cyprus and the Holy Land when the wind was not with us.

It was just as well we hurried; the constant barfing weakened my legs and arms. Strangely enough, the rowing seemed to help just as much as the talking did. Perhaps it distracted me.

We sighted the Syrian coast after a day and a half of hard rowing and a few hours later, the harbour at Latika finally came into view—and not a moment too soon, as far as I was concerned; rowing constantly is a real agony and everyone except William had to row, even me and Reuben and Harold. I had so many blisters on my hands that my blisters had blisters.

But I didn't dare complain and neither did Reuben— everyone had blisters except William and the slaves we freed, whose hands were already callused. William didn't have them because, according to Harold, it is a tradition in England for the highest ranking man on a galley not to row except in the most extreme emergencies.

Latika and its port were pretty much as we'd left them a few weeks earlier except there were now more refugees than ever as a result of the continuing fighting in the interior. The crusaders and the Saracens, it seemed, were going at it tooth and nail in some kind of religious dispute over whose religion was the truth and whose was not.

At least, that's what the priests and bishops said in the churches when they exhorted everyone to join the fight by contributing coins and jewels to support the prayers needed to insure victory.

Apparently, not everyone believed the church's prayers would be answered. Once again a large number of desperate people rushed to the harbour seeking passage—so many people that William ordered only one galley, the one he and I were on, to tie up at the quay.

The other galley stood off about a hundred paces from the quay and periodically used its oars to hold its place in the harbour against the light wind when it gusted. It came in later and moored when we had things on the quay organised.

*****

The scene greeting us on the quay was really quite distressing. There were hundreds and hundreds of refugees and they were desperate to escape. They surged forward as our galley approached and several of them fell into the water.

It was all chaos and shouting as we moored and William took no chances. The pressure from the desperate refugees was so great our men had to draw their swords and stand along the quay and on the deck of our galley to keep people from pushing their way on board.

Even so, several desperate people succeeded in getting past them and jumping down to our deck, including a wild-eyed young girl holding a new born infant. To my surprise, Captain William let her stay aboard when we threw the men back.

It took a while but we finally pushed the noisy and desperate people back far enough and restored a semblance of order. Then some of our sword-carrying men stood along the edge of the quay to keep people from climbing aboard without paying; others surrounded William and me and accompanied us while we tried to find paying passengers and fighting men and sailors to add to our company.

If anything, the crowd of desperate people was even larger and more anxious than the last time we were here.

I really didn't understand why William wanted more sailors and soldiers. They are expensive to feed, you know.

"All archers with their own bows and soldiers with their own swords form a line over by that man," William thundered to the mob in English, and then in French and again in Latin.

He shouted it out to the people on the quay as he pointed to one of the archers who had walked a little ways down the quay and was waving his dirty knitted cap in a circle over his head.

"And everyone with gold and silver coins who wants to buy a passage to Cyprus, form a line by those men over there," he shouted as he pointed to Randolph and a group of our archers and men-at-arms standing near him.

"We'll be taking whoever pays the most to Cyprus. Everyone else must stand back and wait until another galley is available."

With Reuben and I following to act as translators, William first walked over to the archers and men-at-arms forming around Randolph because they wanted to make their marks and join our company. There were two archers with their own longbows and they were immediately accepted. They were from some place I'd never heard of called Wales.

Both of the archers were Welshmen from one of King Richard's mercenary companies. They were, so they claimed, left behind when Richard sailed because they were away delivering a parchment message.

In the end, William let the two archers make their marks to sign into our company along with several others who claimed to be archers and a dozen or so men who had their own swords. Except for men who had the look of veteran sailors and two who claimed to be pilots, he only took men who were carrying their own swords or bows. He rejected all the others, including a number of knights and their men.

Reuben and I translated for Captain William as the knights and their men were turned away. One of the knights he rejected, apparently a German or Swedish crusader, became quite threatening and promptly stomped over to the front of the much larger line of men and women who were trying to buy a passage.

As William finished with his recruiting and our new recruits began making their marks on the parchment contract he had one of our sailors unroll, I walked over to him and quietly pointed out the knight who had made the big fuss when he was rejected as a fighting man.

The German, or whatever he was, had stepped in front of the line of people trying to buy passage and was making trouble by shouting with great rage in his voice and pushing people out of his way.

I asked William what he wanted me to tell Long Bob to do with the knights and soldiers who want to buy passage and looked troublesome.

"Run over and tell Long Bob I said he is to only to accept coins from knights and armed soldiers if they are willing to pay enough—and only if they temporarily surrender their armour, shields, and weapons; and only if they agree to help at the oars along with all the other able-bodied passengers."

So that's what I did. I walked over and gave Bob the message and then walked back to William.

Sure enough, the knight drew himself up quite arrogantly and once again began swearing and shouting threats and waving his sword around when Bob told him the conditions under which he could sail with us.

He was a tall and rather plump and arrogant fellow with a red face, long hair, and a big reddish-blond moustache. He must have been a Templar, or at least wanted to be one, for he smelled as if he had never washed his clothes or wiped his arse.

At first, the knight and Bob could not understand each other. So they moved away from the noisy people standing in line and tried to talk to each other privately. That's when the trouble started.

Before I could get back there one of the men standing closer to them began translating for them—and as he did, the German or whatever he was got more and more excited and threatening.

He apparently got upset when Bob told him he'd not only have to pay and help row, he'd also have to surrender his weapons so we could stow them safely away during the trip.

Hearing Bob say our requirements seemed to tip the knight over the edge. He drew his sword again and began waving it about and raving in a strange guttural language.

The people in the crowd around us went silent, and everyone began backing up and trying to get out of the way.

I watched as Long Bob's archers nocked their arrows and his men-at-arms grasped their swords more firmly and began to lift their shields.

William saw it happening. He quickly finished his business with our new recruits and sent them off to board the galley tied to the quay.

Then he walked down the beach to the knight with his right hand up and open and an inquiring smile on his face as he nodded in agreement—until he reached the man. Then his left hand flashed out from his sleeve and he sank his dagger into the knight's eye up to the hilt.

Good Lord in heaven. He's done it again.

"That is what will happen to any man who tries to threaten or delay the English company and its galleys and cogs from carrying out their duties."

William spoke loudly and was breathing hard as he grasped the handle of the knife in both hands and used it to lower the flailing knight to the ground, despite his death spasms and trembling limbs.

"Tell them what I just said," William ordered me and Reuben as he took a deep breath and gestured toward the people around us.

The crowd was silent as we took turns bellowing out William's words in a number of languages. We received appreciative looks from most of the waiting people as we did; they want to get out of here.

"Get his sword and see if he has a purse and anything else of value," William quietly ordered me as he picked up the knight's sword.

******

My leather bag was once again heavy with coins by the time we finished boarding our paying travellers on our two galleys. They included two French knights and three men-at-arms who had the required amount of coins.

The knights and the men agreed to our terms and their swords and armour were soon in a pile at the front of our galley. They themselves were told to sit far from their weapons on the rowing benches in the rear of the galley near the two rudder men who do the steering.

In addition to the passengers and coins, William was carrying a parchment Reuben asked him to carry back to Aaron. Reuben handed it to me in a leather pouch before he bid us a friendly farewell—and promptly disappeared into the mass of forlorn people who watched us leave.

We got underway and once again we left a large crowd of lamenting and crying people on the shore as our rowing drum began to beat and our oars dug into the water.

******

The good news was that we should make it to Cyprus in fewer hours than it took us to get to Latika—this time we would be using our sails and we had two men at each oar instead of just one of our archers or soldiers.

The men and women who were not rowing and the rest of our passengers were sitting at rest in the aisle running down the centre of the galley between the rowing benches.

The girl with the infant was cowering in the corner next to the rudder men. She looked forlorn and desolate so I gave her part of my loaf and a piece of cheese, and then covered her with my leather rain skin to help keep out the cold.

After we got under way, I realised she might be thirsty and brought her a ladle of water.

Chapter Seven

Yoram the Scribe

Cyprus was just coming into sight in the distance when there was a shout from the front of the galley—something about seeing a galley's sail in the haze ahead of us.

Everyone stood and tried to look forward. A few seconds later we could make out the outline of a galley in the sea haze ahead of us—and it was coming along side some kind of two-masted trading cog and preparing to board it. It was a pirate, for sure, and the cog was its prey.

Captain William and the sergeants began shouting orders, and there was a lot of activity and quite a bit of confusion as our passengers were ordered to man the oars and our fighting men were told to prepare themselves by stringing their bows, unsheathing their swords, and grabbing one of the small galley shields hanging along the rail of the deck.

The weapons and armour of the knights and men-at-arms among our passengers were quickly passed back to them from the front of the galley where they were being stored for safekeeping.

While that was happening, two of the rowing benches were hastily cleared of rowers so sailors could take the rowers' places. They did so and promptly began to carefully coil up the anchor lines and the anchors and prongs they will be using as grappling irons.

I knew all about what our sailors and fighting men were going to do because Captain William had made them practise it at least twice a day, both on the way to Latika and on the way back to Cyprus. But somehow this was different; perhaps because it was real.

From where I was standing I could see the men and passengers of our other galley making the same preparations— and I could look down at the terrified face of the girl with the infant at her breast cowering under the rain hide.

After a few moments of confusion, whilst we got organised, both of our galleys began rowing rapidly towards the beleaguered cog and the pirate galley that had lashed itself to it.

At Captain William's command, some of our archers and fighting men sat down on the rowing benches for the upper tier of oars to help the passengers pull harder.

Our other galley, the one commanded by Randolph, the archer from near London, started forward a few seconds after we did but soon pulled up even with us —probably in response to its slightly faster drum beat and the loud exhortations to its rowers that we could hear drifting over the water to us from Randolph and from Harold who was the sergeant of his sailors.

Of course, Randolph and Harold were hurrying; they were determined not be seen as being late to the fight.

Our galleys sat lower in the water than cogs and the afternoon sun was to the west and behind us. Perhaps that's why the pirates didn't see us until we got fairly close upon them.

I could see the looks of surprise on the pirates' faces when they finally saw us and began to hurriedly re-board their galley. It looked to me to be the Algerian we had seen at Limassol before we left for the Holy Land.

But what do I know? I am not a sailor man.

Our rowing refugee passengers didn't know what to do as we closed on the Algerian and its victim. But many of our men did because we had practised it repeatedly on our voyage from Cyprus.

The rowers on the upper set of oars who would be closest to the pirate galley when we grappled her were pulled out of the way and their places taken by our archers and soldiers.

There was no time for niceties. In some cases, the totally confused passengers on the upper bank of oars were literally pulled out of their seats and thrown aside as our fighting men rushed to take their places on the rowing benches.

Sitting there on the rowing benches meant our men would be able to stand up at the last minute along the rail and fight as soon we came alongside the pirate galley.

Our new men and some of the fighting men travelling as passengers quickly picked up on what our more experienced men were preparing to do. They pushed in to join them and they did so amidst the screams and cries and loudly shouted prayers from many of our paying passengers.

It was a noisy scene of controlled chaos.

******

There was a great grinding crash and the splintering of oars and lots of screams and shouts, both from us and from the pirates, as we came alongside the pirate galley and our sailors threw their grappling irons and pulled us tight against its hull. Even I found myself shouting.

All the while I could look directly across at the nearby pirates in the Algerian galley just as they can look over and see me. I didn't see any archers, thank God.

Standing on the rowing bench next to me was one of Lord William's veteran archers with his longbow. He was shooting arrows as fast as he could nock them, which seemed to me to be very fast indeed.

It was quite fascinating and I remember hearing him grunt every time he shot one of his arrows. What was so fascinating was that he did not pull back on his bow string to shoot—he held the string to his chest and pushed out on the long wooden bow.

The archer's rapid shooting lasted until we banged up against the Algerian galley. He promptly went flying off the rowing seat and stumbled into the men ahead of him, knocking several of them down like bowling pins on the village commons.

But he and the men he knocked down quickly scrambled back to their feet and continued launching their arrows and waving their swords and shouting as they did.

Everywhere there were shouts and screams. The noise was tremendous. But we outnumbered the pirates and surprised them and were fighting according to a plan.

There was a lot of close-quarters fighting as our men and, to a much lesser extent, the pirates stood to arms all along the side where the two galleys were being held together by our grappling lines. I wasn't a fighting man but even I could see how severely our archers were devastating the pirates.

The fighting seemed to go on forever with more and more of our men-at-arms and archers climbing over the side to get on to the deck of the Algerian galley.

Suddenly, it was all over as our other galley succeeded in lashing itself to the other side of the captured cog. Then, with Randolph leading the way, its archers came running across the cog's bobbing deck and began shooting down into the Algerian galley on our side.

The Algerians went down fighting, I'll say that much for them; all of them were killed or wounded, including a few who tried to surrender at the end.

Prize crews and captains were quickly told off for the captured cog and galley and the butcher's bill tallied. Quite a few of our men had cuts and slices, but we lost only two of our new men and three men seriously wounded, including two passengers.

I knew our casualties were called the "butcher's bill" because William used the term when he shouted an inquiry over to Randolph a few minutes later.

The pirates, both dead and wounded, were stripped of their weapons and tossed into the sea at William's orders along with the cog's dead sailors and the bodies of a half dozen or so of the Algerian's galley slaves who, in all the confusion, were mistaken for pirates and killed by our archers and men-at-arms.

Before we got underway, our men searched the captured cog and found three members of its crew still alive. They were hiding in its cargo of olive oil amphoras and corn sacks. At first, they refused to come out because they thought we were pirates. But they soon did and appeared to be greatly appreciative.

I said the men we rescued "appeared to be greatly appreciative" because the sailors who survived looked strange and no one could understand a word they were saying. They must have seen the pirate galley approaching and hid themselves below deck before the pirates began their attack.

We obviously arrived before the pirates had a chance to find them and kill them.

We also freed about forty slaves chained to the Algerian galley's lower tier of rowing benches, including several who were sorely wounded. One of them had an arrow in his side and would surely die.

And wonder of wonders, one of the slaves turned out to be a pock-faced Englishman from one of the villages near the ox fording shallows on the Thames above London. His greying hair and beard hung down beyond his waist. He must have been a captive for many years.

I wonder if he knows Raymond the archer; I heard Raymond tell one of our new men he was a hostler and ox herder before he went for an archer.

******

Our arrival in Limassol with the captured galley and rescued cog caused quite a stir. The men on our anchored cog waved their knitted caps and cheered as we passed by on our way to the quay. Then some of them began piling into the cog's dinghy to come ashore and greet us.

We could also see a large number of people coming out of the city gate and walking and running to the quay as we rowed up to it with the rescued cog in tow. *Yes, I had remembered and reminded William; both of our galleys sailed with a long tow rope.*

Among the crowd of people coming down to the quay to greet us, I was sure, would be Aaron and the other Cyprus merchants coming to find out if we had anything to buy or sell—and most importantly, of course, Father Thomas and young George and the men we left to guard them and work on our fief.

I was not disappointed in my expectations. Merchants and curiosity seekers were still pouring out of the city when I saw Father Thomas and some of our men come around the end of the city wall and hurry down the beach towards us.

It was an altogether happy time. William couldn't contain himself. He jumped on to the quay and grabbed up his son in a big embrace and covered him with kisses. Then he hugged him tightly while he and Father Thomas had a brief conversation.

I watched William and his son from the deck of the galley and thought it quite warming.

A man I'd never seen before was immediately sent running to get wagons to carry our wounded men and to tell Thomas the cook to prepare lots of flatbread and shelters for our wounded and for the new men and refugees.

We had two wagons when we left and now, it seemed, we had four or five—and I knew would soon need even more because we were going to start mining an old ruined building with stone walls on the other side of the city for stones to add to our walls and buildings; I had gone with Father Thomas to look at it before we sailed.

Some of our passengers were already walking into the city to seek food and accommodations. They began leaving while we are still unloading our wounded on to the quay and waiting for wagons to carry them to our fortress.

Others of our passengers, on the other hand, and the galley slaves and survivors from the cog seemed quite dazed. They obviously had no idea where to go or what to do next. They just stood about aimlessly as we helped our wounded men off the boats and on to the quay.

To my surprise and delight, the young girl with the baby was keeping close to me like a starving dog might follow a man carrying newly cooked meat.

When just about everyone was off the boats William, still holding little George, raised his free arm in the air and shouted for everyone to gather around him.

"Everyone who took passage with us and so wishes, including the galley slaves who are all now free, may go into the city as free men, or they may stay with us and work for their food and shelter."

The reactions and looks of relief on the faces of many of the people gathered around William were heart-warming. None more so than those of the young girl standing next to me—she began laughing and crying all at the same time when she heard William say she and her baby would have food and shelter.

She is such a dear little thing. Yes, she is.

******

Everything was fairly well organised by the time the wounded men were loaded on to one of the two wagons. Even the dying galley slave with the arrow in his side was lifted aboard.

I wondered why someone didn't give the galley slave a soldier's "mercy" by chopping his neck with a sword. I'd heard one of the new

archers, who looked at the wounded man as he was being taken off the cog,
comment that men have been known to recover from such wounds, but not
often.

As the wounded were being load, Captain William
announced that Father Thomas would say prayers over the
dead men at the Limassol cemetery that afternoon and all the
wounded would be coming with us for barbering, even the
dying slave with the arrow in his side.

Our sailors and some of the soldiers from among those
who remained ashore during our voyage were ordered to stay
with the boats as guards. Randolph was to be the sergeant in
command of the boats with Harold as his second.

The men named to be the boats' guards were told to bring
our dead men ashore and use the other wagon to take them to
the churchyard for Thomas's prayers and a proper burial. Then
they were to clean the boats and prepare them for another
voyage.

Me? I was walking at the head of the column when we set
out along the track on the beach to walk to our new home.

More precisely, I was walking next to the cart carrying the
wounded men in order to keep a watch on the leather sack with

all the new coins in it—which I'd personally carried off the cog and placed there.

The rest of our party, including most of the freed slaves and the archers and men-at-arms who sailed with us from Latika, were walking behind the cart as we moved toward our new home.

Captain William was still carrying George and he and Father Thomas talked as they walked. Also walking with us were several of the passenger families with children and the young girl with the suckling infant who seemed to have attached herself to me.

Some of our paying passengers apparently used the last of their coins and jewellery to buy their passage and now didn't know what else to do except follow along with us; the girl and the baby, it seemed, had nothing except for each other, and me, of course.

I wonder what William and Thomas will do with the girl and her baby? Surely, they won't sell them as slaves.

******

As we came around the city walls, I could see the roof of our little citadel and the new wall starting to go up around it to improve its defences. It was swarming with men at work.

We'd only been gone for a couple of weeks but there had obviously been a few improvements. The parapets and archers' slits on the west side of the inner wall had been partially repaired, and work had started on the east side and to the north.

Against the west side of the inner wall now stood the biggest change since we left—a number of old and much repaired leather boat sails had been strung over a frame of logs and wood to provide protection from the sun and rain.

Some of our men were obviously living there now instead of everyone crowding into the house or living on the cog and galley we left behind. *I wonder where they got the sails and what they cost?*

Thomas the cook had sheets of flat bread stacked up and more baking on his flattened breastplates when we arrived. A young boy I hadn't seen before was waving a branch over a stack of cheese cuts to keep the flies off.

It was obviously the bread and cheese for tonight's meal and now it was being handed out to our suddenly-hungry men and passengers. I recognised some of the men and women loading the rest of it on to a wagon to take to the men who remained at the harbour with our boats.

******

No one had been particularly hungry on our seasickness-fouled boats but now that we were on shore, we were all thirsty and ravenous with hunger, at least I was; and from the looks of it, so was everyone else.

There was a long line at the barrel of morning ale where another young man I hadn't seen before, a boy actually, was letting everyone have a drink from a ladle he periodically dipped into the barrel to refill.

I took the girl with the infant to the front of the line for a drink, and then to Thomas Cook for some bread and cheese. Thomas cooked delicious flat bread on a couple of knights' breast plates he'd hammered flat and laid across the coals.

******

As soon as we arrived at the old farm-house, I carried the leather coin bag up the new stairs and put its coins into the chests in William and Thomas's room.

They were now so overfull I had trouble shutting one of them. But before I did, I took the girl and her infant to my corner of the downstairs room and pointed to a sleeping hide they could use. I was sure I could find a replacement.

The girl's name, she shyly told me when I asked, was Lena, and whilst we were walking here alongside the wagon, she told me she had named her baby Aria even though she hadn't been baptised yet.

I really didn't know why I was helping her, but somehow her efforts to save the infant and the baby's smile touched my heart. How silly I must look to William and the men.

I'd barely gotten Lena settled in when William called me out. He wanted me to ride with him and young George on the wagon taking food and water down to our boats for the sailors and the fighting men we'd left behind to guard them.

At Father Thomas's insistence, four of the English archers were accompanying us with their bows strung and so were five of our men-at-arms carrying what I later learnt were the new and fearsome bladed pikes our smiths had begun mounting on long poles, almost as soon as we first arrived here.

Father Thomas insisted we be accompanied by armed guards whenever we were outside our little citadel because there had been some trouble involving the local governor while we'd been gone.

I had already gathered as much because I'd heard Thomas and Captain William talking about the King's governor as we followed the food wagon down to the boats—they were discussing whether to kill him now or wait and do it later.

It seemed that while we were gone there had been some trouble with the city's governor, the rather arrogant young knight who accosted Father Thomas in the market when we first arrived.

He apparently had come down from the governor's castle overlooking the city with a number of armed men and visited our new home to demand the payment of a tax.

The King's governor and his men only departed when Father Thomas gulled him with the lie that he had no coins left and couldn't pay him even if he wanted to, because we'd just finished paying the local merchants for the repairs and provisioning of the house and its walls.

Father Thomas also told him that even if there were coins available, which there weren't, no one except Lord William could authorise such a payment for taxes or anything else—if he wanted coins he would have to wait and ask William for them.

Apparently, after a few relatively tense minutes, the King's governor turned away and marched his men back to his castle on the hill above Limassol—but only after Father Thomas assured him that in a few days William would be returning from the Holy Land and might have acquired coins which could be used to pay the governor's tax.

We all laughed when, with a twinkle in his eye, Thomas dryly added that the sight of so many armed men inside our headquarters and its repaired and strengthened walls might have also entered into governor's decision to go away and come back later.

It also might have been, Thomas suggested wryly, the fact many of the governor's men-at-arms appeared to be peasants newly arrived from France who had never been learnt to use the weapons they were carrying.

******

Men came in from the boats and began gathering about the food wagon as soon as we arrived back at the quay.

Normally, the men on the boats took turns walking up to the cookhouse each morning and evening to fetch their meals and a cup of the ale Andrew the brewer had started making. Not this day.

Coming to the cookhouse for food when the sun finished passing over the earth and darkness fell would continue, of course, but this food was primarily for the new men and the sailors who had just arrived with us and were staying on the boats. They were appreciative and ate ravenously.

Whilst the men were eating, Thomas and William talked to the archer sergeant, Andrew, who does the brewing, and the men who had been left under his command to guard the farm-house and boats when we sailed last week. They had nothing special to report.

To the contrary, except for the governor's visit, everything in the city seemed quiet and normal. At least, that was the word from the women from the taverns and brothels who'd come on board to please the men, and didn't seem to be interested in much except spreading their legs to earn some coins. *No surprise there.*

******

Before we left to walk down to our boats moored at the quay, William had me get a little sack of coins from one of the chests. Now George was handing them out—ten copper coins for every man who fought. He called it "prize money" and said five were for the pirate galley and five were for the cog. He also brought gold bezants so he could give two to each of the families of our three men and passengers who had been killed or seriously wounded in the fighting.

"This is my son," William told our new men by way of explanation as George, with a serious look on his face, carefully counted ten copper coins into the hands of every man who had taken up arms against the Algerian pirates.

"I want him to understand why men who do their duty must always be quickly recognised and rewarded."

I was quite surprised at how responsive and gentle the hard-bitten men were as the boy carefully counted out the coins into their hands. I was also surprised to learn that neither of William's two new men who were killed had families to claim their death coins. It's very sad, not having a family.

Chapter Eight

Three days after we returned from Syria, William ordered me
and a number of archers and men-at-arms to accompany Father
Thomas on a march to Nicosia. We were going to pay homage
to Guy of Lusignon, the French lord who was the newly
crowned King of Cyprus.

*Why are we doing this? Something is up. But what is it? And why
haven't we heard any more from the local governor?*

Everyone in Christendom knew about Cyprus's hapless
King Guy. He'd succeeded Baldwin and been the bumbling
Christian king in Jerusalem until he was captured by Saladin—
after leading his men to an absolutely disastrous and
unnecessary defeat at the battle of Hattin.

Hattin is where most of Guy's men were killed and the rest
died of thirst because he led them to a battle in a place where
there was no water—and, unlike the Saracens, he hadn't
thought to arrange any for his men.

The crusader nobles so feared Guy's incompetence they
didn't want him to return to Jerusalem as king when Saladin
finally released him for a ransom.

Then, in a compromise to end a possible civil war between the French crusaders supporting Guy and all the others, Guy was allowed to buy Cyprus from the Templars and proclaim himself to be its king.

Because he was the King and we intended to remain here, Father Thomas and I were going to pay homage to him. At least that's why I thought we were going to see him.

******

Father Thomas was quite talkative on our trek, and I learnt a many things about William and the archers.

"William and I are quite fortunate the archers contracted with Lord Edmund after Richard left instead of contracting to stay with King Guy in Jerusalem. Otherwise we'd probably have died at Hattin along with the rest of his army.

"Guy is well born and extremely limited as is strangely the case with many nobles because of their weak blood—he governed Jerusalem so badly his people revolted and he led his men into battle so stupidly he got most of them killed at Hattin and the rest died in the desert from lack of water."

Based on what little I knew about his governor in Limassol, the King also didn't know how to pick his sergeants very well either. Once again I wondered why we hadn't heard from the King or the governor since William and I returned?

******

Our arrival in Nicosia created quite a stir. The lookouts on the citadel next to the city gate must have seen the dust raised by our party. They sounded the alarm and closed the gates.

The dust and the alarm dissipated when our men sat on the ground to rest while Father Thomas and I continued on alone until we reached the closed city gate. The good Father and I were many things, but we didn't look dangerous.

"Who are you and what do you want?" demanded the sergeant of the guards who came out through the door in the gate to surround us.

Father Thomas looked at the sergeant of the guards rather arrogantly and announced himself. *He did being arrogant quite well, by the way.*

"I am Father Thomas, and we are ambassadors representing Lord William, Admiral of the English Fleet. We are here to speak with King Guy and pay homage to him." *Admiral? Well, I suppose he is.*

"What do you want to speak to him about?"

"That is the King's business and certainly none of yours," Thomas said rather pompously, with a disdainful snap to his voice.

"Please inform His Majesty that we are here and most respectfully request an audience at his earliest convenience."

The sergeant captain of the guards who bustled up in response to the sergeant's shout was perplexed and clearly not quite sure how to respond or what to do.

He doesn't know what to do when someone claiming to be an ambassador arrives and asks to see the King? This man is either very new to his job or seriously stupid.

****** *Yoram*

We were allowed to enter the city gate through a little door cut into it. Then, after being searched for weapons and none being found, we stood in the sun by the city wall to warm ourselves while one of the guards hurried away to report our arrival.

Father Thomas looked on in amusement when I took advantage of the wait to piss against the wall. Then he shrugged his shoulders and did the same. *Who knows when we might have another opportunity?*

After a while, a grey-haired, older man with a self-important look on his face bustled up in a highly decorated robe. Without identifying himself, he demanded, in Latin, to know who we are and what we want.

Once again, Father Thomas announced us as ambassadors from Lord William, Admiral of the English Fleet, presently at anchor in Limassol, and here to pay homage to the King.

"And to discuss certain matters of state and finance that might be of mutual benefit and enrichment for the King and the Admiral."

Well, that got the man's attention. I wonder who he is.

"What matters of state and finance? You must tell me about the matters you wish to discuss before you can be allowed to meet with His Majesty—I am Lord Alstain, the King's Chamberlain and head of the King's council."

Lord Alstain emphasised the word "before." *Ah. He wants a bribe.* Father Thomas picked up on it immediately.

"Our news is quite pleasant, and we would be most pleased to share it with you, Lord Alstain, except we are under the strictest of orders from our liege lord, Admiral William of England, to only share our news with King Guy.

"Your assistance in our having a successful meeting with the King would, of course, be greatly valued, particularly if we are able to establish a mutually beneficial relationship between the King and our liege lord." *We'll pay you, but only if all goes well.*

A few minutes later, Lord Alstain led us into a totally empty room and told us to wait. After he left, a skinny girl wearing a patched and dirty gown, undoubtedly a slave, came in and handed each of us a bowl of refreshing red wine.

Then Father Thomas and I were left alone for hours, so long that we both needed chamber pots—and none were on offer.

Finally I went to the entrance to the room and spoke to the guard standing there. He didn't understand at first, but he finally did when I pretended to piss and poop. He shouted something down the corridor.

A few minutes later, the same skinny girl who'd brought us the wine carried in a smelly wooden bowl, obviously a chamber shite pot that someone else had recently used. It was a great relief for both of us.

About an hour later, we were conducted into the presence of the King with great ceremony. The chamberlain, for that is how Alstain titled himself to us, led us down a long corridor and into a big room with a finely dressed man sitting on an elevated chair at the other end. People, mostly men but a few surprisingly well-dressed women, were standing on either side of the room.

Everyone seemed quite curious and watched closely as we walked between them towards the sitting man. He was undoubtedly King Guy.

We could see everyone in the room quite clearly because it was lit by the sun coming through some kind of clear glass that covered the wall openings, just like it did in one of the churches I visited in Damascus with the Bishop.

Ah, and there is the pudgy, young, French knight who is the governor of Limassol. Well, that explains why we haven't heard from him for a while. Perhaps he's been recalled or is here asking for instructions.

I walked somewhat behind Father Thomas with my eyes down and copied him when he bowed and prostrated himself on his belly in front of the King.

As you might imagine, I had never seen a king before. But this poor fellow must have been very insecure, for he seemed quite pleased by our extremely submissive behaviour.

We scrambled to our feet and stood as supplicants with our heads down when the King motioned for us to stand up. I could see him out of the corner of my eye. He looked to be a rather tall, good-looking man of middle age wearing some kind of gold band around his head.

"I am told you wish to speak with us." *Us?* He spoke in French.

"Yes, your esteemed Royal Highness and Majesty," Father Thomas explained in French after we jumped to our feet.

"I am Father Thomas, the head priest of the English Navy, and I am here as the ambassador of my liege lord, Admiral Lord William of England, to pay homage and be submissive to you in his name.

"As I'm sure you know, Your Esteemed Majesty, at the personal request of the Pope, Admiral William and his men have been rescuing people fleeing the Saracens and carrying them to Limassol. I am happy to report that many of the refugees are spending their coins in Limassol so as to enrich that city's merchants. That will, of course, enhance the ability of Your Esteemed Majesty's governor to collect taxes from them.

"Admiral William and his men, I am also happy to report to Your Majesty, are further enriching Your Esteemed Majesty's kingdom by spending the coins they receive from the grateful refugees to buy supplies from your merchants and to repair ruined buildings to shelter themselves and the refugees."

The King nodded.

"Yes, we have heard of these good things about the Lord Admiral and we welcome him to our realm."

"Thank you, Your Esteemed Majesty, God will surely bless you."

Now comes the gulling.

"Ahem," Father Thomas continued after clearing his throat.

"As you are undoubtedly aware, Your Esteemed Majesty, King Richard of England is missing. This has caused unexpected problems both for my Lord Admiral and for the humble priests such as myself who serve him and his men and all Christians sailing on God's seas and oceans.

"It seems, quite unfortunately of course, that missing with Richard and his court are the patents of nobility from a Christian king my Lord Admiral needs in order to impress the local lords when his galleys and cogs arrive in heathen ports to retrieve their refugees and carry them to safety.

"Indeed, I myself am missing the appointment letters as the Bishop of Bekka carried by the papal nuncio accompanying Richard."

"I see. Yes, I can see how that might make things difficult," the King said nodding his head.

I am glad he sees; I certainly don't.

"It would mean a great deal to my Lord Admiral, and Christians everywhere, and to me and the Pope and the Church as well," Father Thomas replied, "if Your Illustrious Majesty would use his kingly powers to help rectify the problems caused by the disappearance of King Richard and the Pope's legate."

Then Father Thomas explained what he wanted.

"As I am sure you know, Your Majesty, Admiral William has set aside three hundred gold coins, every one of them a bezant from Constantinople, to cover the expenses of recovering the missing parchments.

"I am sure he'd be willing to use them to cover any expenses that you as a king with the same powers as Richard might bear in providing suitable alternatives—so Admiral William's efforts to assist Christian pilgrims might occur more quickly and have a better outcome.

"Similarly available, of course, are the one hundred gold coins the Lord Admiral set aside for recovering or replacing the documents from Richard's papal nuncio related to my appointment as the Bishop of Bekka."

We'll bribe you both.

The King pondered what he'd heard for a moment, looked a bit confused, and glanced at his chamberlain, who nodded and came to the King and whispered in his ear. Then the King came through for us.

"Rest assured, good priest. We are always willing to take steps to help the Church and good Christians such as you and the Lord Admiral."

I am willing to make a deal.

"Your Majesty's generosity and goodness is so well known and the need of the Church and the Christian refugees is so great and immediate that I took the liberty of preparing the necessary documents for Your Royal Highness's consideration and seal. As well, of course, as those for your papal nuncio's seal for matters related to the English Fleet."

With that, Father Thomas fell again to his knees and put his forehead on the stone floor as he held out the two parchment rolls I had scribed for him with great flourishes on all the letters. He held them out not to the King, of course, but to the side for one of the courtiers to take and carry to the King. I, of course, copied Thomas and fell to my knees and banged my head on the floor when he did.

How strange. The weather's fairly warm today but the stones feel cold as ice.

We bowed continuously and profusely as we backed out of the King's presence.

The King's chamberlain bowed and backed out with us and, once outside and out of earshot of the King's courtiers, enthusiastically congratulated Father Thomas on doing such a good job of handling the King.

Then he told us he would let us know when the documents were signed and sealed but, quite unfortunately, he would need to convince the King to sign them so there could be a delay of a few days, or perhaps even longer. He had no idea how long it would take.

It will only happen if I get paid.

Father Thomas responded that we would greatly value the chamberlain's assistance. He informed Lord Alstain that we would return to Limassol and await the King's decision.

Then Thomas carefully assured the chamberlain he would personally convey the coins for the expenses of the King and his papal nuncio to Nicosia as soon as we heard that the parchments were signed and ready to be picked up.

"And, of course, with some additional coins for you to cover the expenses of your assistance in obtaining the necessary signatures and seals."

You'll get paid when we get the signed and sealed parchments.

The two men nodded and smiled at each other profusely; an agreement had been reached between gentlemen.

Father Thomas and I talked quietly as one of the King's servants led us back to the city gate.

"Will the King really put his seal to them and the nuncio too? Is it possible?" I asked.

"Oh, I should think so. The King needs money, many bags of money, to regain the throne of Jerusalem which is the throne he really wants.

"He's obviously comfortable with the buying and selling of titles since he bought Cyprus from the Templars; and he's probably a bit short of coins at the moment since the Templars no doubt took him for all he had.

"They were greedy little buggers, you know, the Templars are—in addition to being good soldiers and filthy, because they proudly never wash themselves or their clothes—they have got it in their minds that Jesus was a god and never had to wipe his arse, don't they?"

Chapter Nine

Sergeant *Yoram*

"Did he go for it?"

Those were the first words an anxious and hot and sweaty William asked Father Thomas as we approached him in the courtyard. He asked as we stood watching the master joiner's men sway a trimmed log into place. It would be part of a barracks and stable being built all along the inside of the new wall.

Some of the stalls would be used for our horses; some for our fighting men and the families they would inevitably form if we stayed here permanently. They would replace the current sail-covered tent shelters our men were using, hopefully before they blew away again, as they did in the storm several weeks ago.

"I think so," Father Thomas answered.

"But we won't know for sure until we get the word. So tell me little brother, how is our George and what has happened since we left?"

"George is up the stairs taking a nap. He's fine. Eating like a horse as always, isn't he?"

Then, with a big and triumphant smile, William made an announcement.

"The big news I have, brother dear, is that we have received this morning an offer from Aaron and the Limassol merchants to buy both of our cogs and the cargo of olive oil and corn in the one we captured."

William said it with a big smile as he rubbed his fingers together to indicate a merchant counting coins.

"It seems," William continued, "Aaron and a group of the local merchants want to buy both cogs, put an additional cargo of oil and corn in the empty one we bought off the poxed captain, and pay us to convoy both of the cogs to Alexandria with our three galleys acting as their guards."

Then he told us all about it.

"They started by offering two hundred Damascus gold bezants; we reached an agreement two hours ago for three hundred and twenty.

"Half of the coins are already upstairs in the chests. We'll receive the other half when we are ready to sail—and, if you can believe it, they'll take all the risk of losing the cargos to pirates so long as only our men and theirs' are on board the cogs and our galleys convoy them."

William is obviously pleased with himself, and, it would appear, rightly so. We are going to need another coin chest.

"Do we have enough men to crew two cogs and three galleys and still leave enough good men here with you to guard this place and my son?" William asked with a sigh.

Then he answered his own question.

"No. Not by half. So long as the coins and George are here we'll always need to have a hundred or more of our best men here to guard them including most of the English archers. It means we must recruit another couple of hundred fighting men for our company and, if we can buy or make enough longbows, apprentice some of them to train to be archers."

"You're right, William," Father Thomas agreed. "We'll have to scour Cyprus for men and weapons, and you'll probably have to make another trip to Syria, or maybe even to Acre, to recruit more men and paying passengers before we can risk a voyage to Alexandria with the cogs."

"Well, that might do, my dear priestly brother; yes, it might. We can look for men and try to buy weapons while we wait to hear what the King does about the documents."

And that's what we decided to do. And I was quite pleased when they asked for my opinion so I could agree with them.

******

Captain William stood with his brother and me at the gate the next morning as we watched small recruiting parties of our men walk out of our bustling camp. Each of them was heading to one of Cyprus's five other walled cities and the villages that surrounded it. Their job was to encourage men to come here and apply to join our company.

Our recruiters would, everyone hoped, evaluate the abilities and potential of the men before they encouraged them to come and apply. That explained why each of the recruiting parties was commanded by one of the English archer sergeants and included one or more of our brighter and more experienced new men as his second.

More specifically, each of our recruiting parties was to encourage all the fit and experienced archers and soldiers they could find to come to Limassol and apply to join our company. They'd been told to particularly look for men who already had their own weapons, since they were the ones most likely to know how to use them.

Anyone the recruiters found with his own weapons, if they came to Limassol and were approved by the Captain, would be allowed to make their mark on the company's contract and get the same food and one gold coin per year as everyone else.

Our recruiting parties were also to recruit strong young men on a food and clothing basis for training as apprentice archers, particularly those with good legs, good eyesight and teeth, and strong arms who might, with practise, become strong enough to push an arrow out of an English archer's longbow.

We met with the recruiting sergeants the night before they left. There were enough questions to make my head spin.

"And what if they have women and want to bring them?" asked Simon, one of the archer sergeants, a bearded Englishman from Surrey with a particularly fine longbow.

Captain William and Father Thomas just looked at each other. Finally, the Captain made a decision.

"The experienced men who bring their own weapons can also bring their women; we'll feed the women and their children if they'll work at our camp in the kitchen or fletching arrows or on the walls. The women of the men who come to be apprentice archers will have to wait at home until their men are trained and allowed to make their marks on the company's roll."

"Knights?" one of the other sergeants asked. "What do we do if a knight wants to join us, William?"

"You know better than that, Archie," was William's reply, said with a touch of exasperation in his voice. "No knights; it's in our contract, isn't it?"

That's not surprising; according to a conversation I had with Randolph, knights are often too arrogant to take orders from common archers and often don't get along well with others.

"How soon will we have someone in the markets to buy weapons and how much will we pay?"

"That's a good question, Robert, a very good question. We'll start buying them rather quickly if the prices are right. The next week or two, I should think."

I hope it will be me who does the buying. Then maybe I can stay here and take care of Lena and Aria instead of going on the next voyage.

"Slaves? What about slaves and serfs, William? Should we offer to buy any if they look good?"

"You can bring in any serfs who look good and want to run. But we are not buying any slaves, Simon. Never. And don't sign up any who approach you about running away to join us—unless they speak English.

"English-speaking slaves are different. Always inquire about them and their whereabouts when you talk to people.

Let it be known that we always reward people who tell us about English-speaking slaves and we always, absolutely always, cut the bollocks and dingles off anyone who owns them or mistreats them.

"But don't take chances if you see or hear of any English-speaking slaves. Come back here if you see or hear of any and we'll go out in force to bring them in."

******

After we watched our recruiting parties depart, William turned to young George and asked him if he'd like to go with him out to our boats while he told Randolph and the sergeant captains and men on the boats what to do if any serfs and slaves showed up.

"Hoy there, George, would you like to go with me and Yoram out to the boats while I visit with your Uncle Randolph to make sure our sailors are alright and talk to him about some things? Afterwards we'll go to the market to visit Aaron the corn merchant.

"You remember Aaron, don't you, George? He's the nice man who gave you an apple and let you ride on his shoulders when he came to visit us a couple of days ago."

George was quite enthusiastic about visiting the boats and the market so we all walked down to the beach to visit Randolph and his men. A couple of our boats' dinghies were pulled up on the sand, so we didn't even have to hail the boats to have someone row in to get us.

Randolph and his sergeant captains saw us coming in one of the dinghies and were waiting expectantly as we climbed aboard the nearest galley.

"How are things going, Randolph?"

"Good William; things are good, thankee. We are ready to sail any time you give the word. But we'll need to take on more food and water if we are to go beyond Latika or bring back a full load of recruits and refugees."

"You're right and thank you for reminding me. The galleys may go out but don't worry about the cogs, at least not for a while. We don't know when the cogs will sail but, when they do, it looks like we'll be using the galleys to convoy them all the way to Alexandria with cargos of olive oil and corn, maybe wine too.

"Our problem, of course, is that we don't have enough sailors and fighting men. We've got to find more men first."

"Aye, Captain, that's the talk I heard when I was ashore for breakfast this morning. Do you want me to bring the cog we took off the Algerians to the quay so it can be loaded?"

Nothing is secret around here. I need to remember that.

"Not yet. George and I are off to the market to see the merchants so I'll let you know how soon it will be when you come ashore for supper tonight. But it probably won't be immediately—we can't leave until we have enough men both for the galleys and cogs and to stay here and defend our new fortress."

"Aye, so I hear. Well, there is one thing we'uns will need if we are to go to Alexandria with more than one galley—pilots who knows the way. Naught but Harold knows how to pilot us from here to there."

"Pilots? By God, you're right," was William's response.

"We'll need one for each galley in case they get separated," he said. "Thank you for reminding me. I'll ask the merchants. Maybe they'll know of some pilots."

Randolph absolutely beamed when William acknowledged his idea. *I've got to remember to praise the men when they make good suggestions and accomplish things.*

******

Aaron's stall was in one of the busiest sections of the
Limassol market, the lane where the dealers in cooking oil and
corn ply their trade. Large amphora jars of oil and sacks of
corn were stacked in his stall and piled high in the yard behind
it.

Several women were standing in front of his stall with pots
and gourds. They were obviously there to buy supplies for
their households.

One of the men working in Aaron's stall, a heavyset man
with greying hair, saw us approaching and shouted something
over his shoulder in a strange language. Aaron himself came
bustling around the corner a few seconds later with a big smile
on his face and greeted us most effusively in Latin.

"It is good to see you, Captain William and you, Father
Thomas, and you too, young George and Sergeant Yoram. *Yes,
I'm a sergeant now.* Please join me for some wine or tea and tell
me about your good health and how your compound is
progressing. Everyone says your men are doing a splendid job
and it's coming along nicely."

Aaron promptly gobbled some instructions to the heavyset
man in a language I didn't understand and motioned for us to

follow him through his stall to a low table in a shaded part of his storage yard.

We had no more than exchanged pleasantries and begun to seat ourselves on the pillows around the table when a skinny young man from a nearby food stall rushed in with a skin of wine, some wooden bowls, and a tray of dates and sliced oranges.

A few seconds later, two men I hadn't met before appeared, both obviously merchants, greeted us effusively, and sat down with us.

"My partners for the shipment of oil and corn to Alexandria," Aaron explained as he introduced them to William and the rest of us as Tramon and Leon, corn merchants.

Behind them a young man appeared with a tray of olives, and figs, and then another arrived with tea and pieces of cheese and dainty little bowls the likes of which I've never seen.

We are getting the full and proper attention due valuable customers, and rightly so; this is big business and our custom is valued.

We constantly waved our hands to distract the flies as we began exchanging pleasantries, and the men vied with one another to entertain little George by slicing fruit and cheese for him and squeezing lemons into his water bowl.

Only when George ran off to play with some boys in the market did we get down to talking seriously. Our tablemates, of course, wanted to know how soon they must have their cargo assembled and to the quay for loading.

"Two weeks, and perhaps more than that," William told them. His response drew looks of relief from the men.

They are obviously still organising the additional oil and corn for the second cog. And perhaps some wine too, since some of Aaron's friends sitting with us were named as wine merchants.

"We won't go until we finish recruiting more sailors and fighting men, both for crews and to defend our base here. The stronger our force, the less likely that pirates will try to take the cogs and their cargo."

"That is twice good news, Admiral William. And I am glad to hear we'll have a few more weeks. It will give us more time to find the most profitable cargo to send. We have the wine and corn from last year's crop, of course, but most of the olives are not yet quite ready to be harvested and pressed."

I wonder how they know about the "Admiral" in Admiral William? They must have someone in the King's court.

William got down to business with his response.

"As you probably know, my friends, we've sent recruiting parties across the island to find experienced soldiers and archers to add to our company for the trip to Alexandria with your goods. And a few more sailors and pilots wouldn't be amiss.

"Frankly, I am not optimistic about finding many more fighting men on Cyprus, although, we may be able to recruit some from among the King's men in Nicosia. So I am seriously thinking about making a quick trip back to Latika with two of our galleys, and perhaps on to Acre as well."

Then William added a bit of an explanation.

"I believe we might be able to find experienced fighting men and more sailors in the cities and among the refugees."

And, of course, although William didn't say it, if we go we may find more refugees willing to pay to escape to Cyprus.

"If I decide to go back to the Holy Land, which is how I am leaning at the moment, the third galley and most of our men will stay here to help guard your cogs and my compound."

"Yes, Admiral, we have heard about the recruiting parties you sent out. I, for one, am pleased to know that our cogs and their cargo will be so well guarded."

The others nodded enthusiastically and added their agreement.

I bet they are most pleased of all that Father Thomas and George will remain here if William sails. It is a surety that William will not just sail away with their cargo and the cogs they are buying from us.

Everyone around the little table leaned forward and listened intently as William raised the possibilities of new opportunities.

"There are other things we might be able to do together, beyond the guarding of cargo boats and carrying parchment merchant orders and payment coins for you.

"For instance, we need to buy weapons for the apprentice archers we will be recruiting, even though they will not be going to Alexandria—bows, particularly longbows and crossbows, as well as swords, metal arrow tips, strong bow strings, and wood that my men and their women can work into bows and shafts for our pikes and arrows."

What followed was a lot of discussion on many topics: about prices and commissions for supplies and weapons; where else the Limassol and Latika merchants do business and how they might use our galleys to convoy their cargos in the future or carry parchments and coins; about how soon Latika and Acre would fall to the Saracens; and where else the merchants thought our company of English archers might find it profitable to set up fortified compounds similar to the one we were establishing in Limassol.

"What we are looking for, William told them, are ports where we might safely gather cargos and passengers so they'd be ready to sail when our galleys arrive to carry them or escort them.

It was all quite interesting—particularly when the discussion turned to the possible use of heavily armed war galleys such as ours to carry the merchants' parchment messages and coin payment orders to other cities. The merchants were keen on the possibility that they would not have to risk sending their payment coins by sea where the pirates might get them.

I believe I understand how it might work but I am not sure. I think it would require holding a supply of coins in each of our posts to pay the parchment payment orders that arrive—and that could attract robbers and pirates and greedy officials. It would be dangerous without a proper fortress and guards in each port to keep them out.

*****

The next morning, William ordered me go to the market to confirm to Aaron and the merchants his decision to take two of our galleys on another trip to Latika, and possibly on to Acre.

"My decision should please them. It will give them more time to gather their goods together—and give us a chance to carry more passengers and recruit more sailors and fighting men to protect their cargos."

The big and quite distressing news, at least so far as I was concerned, was that I was to go with him. Lena gasped and was quite distressed when I told her. *Her reaction pleased me immensely; she's become very dear to me.*

In any event, we would leave the next day on the morning wind and return in a week or two, depending on the weather. Father Thomas and young George would remain here.

One galley would also remain here with a full crew of fighting men on board, with Raymond in overall command both on land and sea. It would be his job to fight off any pirates who might try to take our cogs and to help in the fight if our compound is attacked by the governor or anyone else. Harold would command the galley on which William and I would be sailing.

Perhaps I looked unhappy when I heard the news because William hastened to explain to me why our galleys were not likely to be attacked even if they sailed with partial crews—because they would have no cargo and everyone on board would be a fighting man.

I thanked him most profusely for the reassurance—and didn't tell him my unhappiness was about leaving Lena and the baby.

The fact was that I've been increasingly concerned ever since Lena told me her baby was a girl and shyly asked me if I thought Aria was an acceptable name. And I got even more concerned when she asked me if I thought Father Thomas would be willing to baptise the baby even though her husband was dead and she had no man to stand up for her.

I was quick to tell Lena that Aria sounded like a fine name and she smiled shyly and nodded her agreement when I offered my services at the baptism—that's why I went straightaway to speak with Father Thomas about baptising the infant and protecting her while I was away.

Father Thomas nodded sagely when I explained the situation.

"Of course she should be baptised," was his immediate response. But then he told me about the problem.

"There is a problem because the child's father is dead— someone must take primary responsibility for her religious upbringing and at least one other man must be available as her godfather in the event the first man fails or falls. And all of them must be men the mother will accept.

"Will she accept you and William for such important roles?"

Would Captain William really be Aria's godfather if I asked him?

"Do you think Captain William would do that?" I asked Father Thomas. Then, I explained.

"Lena said she would be pleased if I took the father's role and it would please me to do it. But do you really think the Captain might be willing to be the child's godfather?"

Father Thomas just smiled and suggested I ask him. So that is what I did when I returned from telling Aaron that two of our galleys would be leaving tomorrow for another voyage to Latika and, perhaps, to Acre.

What happened next truly surprised me: William agreed to be Aria's godfather and that afternoon all the original archers and many of the new men gathered around as I held little Aria and Father Thomas baptised her.

Lena pleased me greatly by clinging to me with tears in her eyes throughout the ceremony, and the men all nodded and murmured their agreement when Father Thomas asked if they too would stand up for the child Aria and help her when she needed help. Truth be told, I felt quite emotional and had tears in my eyes when it was all over.

Then everyone gathered around to gently touch the child and kiss Lena on the cheek and clap me on the shoulder.

We all laughed when Aria's tiny little hand closed around one of rough old Long Bob's fingers and melted his heart when she held it.

"Blimey, she's got me," he said in wonderment.

******

Our plan was to go out tomorrow on the morning wind with about sixty fighting men and sailors on each galley, even though sixty men was not even enough men to fully man all the oars.

We were taking so few men because we didn't expect to be attacked—and going out lightly manned would give us more room for new recruits and paying passengers.

But sailing for the Holy Land the next day was not to be. Everything changed late in the afternoon when a horseman from the King's chamberlain appeared at the gate to our fortress with a message saying the documents were ready in Nicosia. *That was quick.*

Father Thomas and Captain William were elated and our plans quickly changed. Instead of rowing out or sailing on the morning wind, Father Thomas and I and half the archers and swordsmen in the crews of the two galleys, well over one hundred men, were on our way to Nicosia with a mule carrying six small sacks of gold and silver coins for the King and a smaller pouch for the chamberlain.

The men would board their galleys and we would head for Latika and the Holy Land as soon as we returned. We probably didn't need so many men but William insisted we take them because "it will send a message to the King and his courtiers about our strength."

****** *Yoram*

We made good time on the cart path to Nicosia, and even ran into several of our recruiting parties coming back along the track in the other direction.

The party coming from Nicosia had done particularly well. It had almost forty recruits with it including some dozen or more experienced archers and soldiers who, the recruiting party's sergeant took us aside and warned us privately, were probably deserters from the King's guard who left with their weapons.

On the second day of walking along the track to Nicosia, who should we find coming towards us on the back of a mule with a large party of guards and a big smile on his face and our parchment documents all signed and sealed—the King's chamberlain himself, Lord Alstain.

The chamberlain obviously wants to get his hands on the bezants before the King sees them—which I'm sure will be fine with Father Thomas so long as he gets the signed and sealed documents.

Examining the documents and their seals and then exchanging them for the gold bezants took only a matter of minutes, particularly after Father Thomas loudly asked me if I have the sack with the gold coins for the chamberlain to cover his expenses.

On the face of things, the chamberlain was behaving properly and we would end up with what we want.

But why did he come to meet us?

I couldn't contain myself once the deal was done and we turned around to begin our walk back along the dusty track to Limassol.

"Why did he come to meet us, Father Thomas . . . uh, I mean Bishop Thomas?"

"I've been wondering about that myself. He probably wanted to steal some of the King's coins. But it really doesn't matter; we drafted the documents and the seals of the King and the papal nuncio look genuine, so it doesn't matter who ends up with the coins."

Chapter Ten

Sergeant *Yoram*

A day and a half later, the rowing drums began beating and our two galleys finally got underway for Latika and the Holy Land. We were going out on the morning wind of a hot summer day without a cloud in the sky; the rowers were sweating before we even cleared the harbour.

I dread having to take my turn at the oars; my hands are still blistered from the last time.

We were going out with our galley crews severely under strength, both so we would have more room for paying passengers when we returned and so enough of our most experienced and dependable fighting men could be left behind to defend our boats and our little citadel.

We didn't expect our galleys to be attacked even if we ran into pirates—we were in war galleys and all of the men in the two crews except for me and a few of the sailors were experienced fighting men. And perhaps more importantly, we had nothing of value on board to interest pirates.

Whilst we were gone, the men we left behind under Father Thomas and Randolph would keep working to strengthen the headquarters fort and begin training our new recruits.

Also, and something new and important, an arrow-making workshop was to be set up with Brian, the wounded archer, as its sergeant. The barber dug the arrow out of Brian's leg and he seemed to be recovering although he was now walking with a limp and a pain that seemed to be worse than ever.

Poor Athol, on the other hand, still only looked off with a blank stare despite all the bleeding the barber had been doing. Even the potions administered by Limassol's Greek doctor didn't help him.

Harold, the red-haired former slave with the scarred face, was the sergeant captain of our galley and its pilot. He'd been to Latika before and apparently knew the way.

Randolph, the archer who was the master sergeant of all our boats, was staying in Limassol with Henry to help supervise the archery training of our new recruits. He would command the men and sergeants on the cogs and the galley which remain behind.

All the arrangements had been made before Father Thomas and I got back from delivering the gold bezant coins to the chamberlain. So I wasn't sure who had been appointed the sergeant captain of the other galley or if it had its own pilot.

I hope they have their own pilot or they might not find their way if we get separated. It's worrisome because that galley cost many coins and we only just bought it off its poxed captain a month or so ago. I'll have to remember to ask Captain William.

******

Our galleys each hung a candle lantern on their mast that night and the next. And it worked—the weather wasn't bad at all and the galleys were able to keep each other in sight throughout the night. It enabled our fast-moving galleys to travel together for the entire trip.

We saw only one sail, a Venetian cog, on the first two days and, of course, nothing at night since only war galleys and guarded convoys would dare show lights in these pirate-infested waters.

When the sun came up on the third day, we were near the coast of the Holy Land. That's when we finally began seeing sails in the distance.

What we saw were cogs and fishing boats, some of them quite small, but not a single war galley. Several of the cogs turned tail and ran as soon as they saw us. William totally ignored them.

I was much relieved; that's when I knew for sure I wasn't going to be in a company of pirates.

Unfortunately, despite the good weather and visibility, the winds and currents pushed us further south than we intended. And then Harold compounded the problem by turning us to run further south along the coast. We were half way to Acre before Harold realised he'd made a mistake and admitted the problem.

I wonder if Harold really is a pilot or if he was just pretending? William seems to trust him, however, and that's what counts.

At that point, everything changed. William decided Acre, the heavily fortified and most important port in the Holy Land, would be our first port of call instead of Latika.

Acre, William told me, was a place he and the archers knew well. They'd been here a few years back under King Richard when he starved-out the Saracen defenders and took the city's great fort—and, in capturing it, disgraced himself and caused the archers to contract to follow Lord Edmond to the Bekka Valley to help defend his crusader castle.

"What Richard did was kill his Saracen prisoners, despite giving his word he would not. His perfidy infuriated Saladin and caused him to launch great attacks on Christians everywhere.

"It also disgusted the archers in our company and caused us to leave Richard's service when our contract expired. We left Richard and contracted with Lord Edmund to help defend his crusader castle and lands in the Bekka Valley."

That's when I learnt William and Father Thomas and all the English were touchy about people who don't keep their word, even though the prisoners were only useless heathens and undoubtedly deserved to die.

******

There were many boats and boats of all types and sizes moored to the harbour's stone quay and along the wooden wharves running in front of the great Acre Fortress of the crusaders. It was truly an impressive fortress with its many banners stitched with the insignia of the Order of the Knights of Saint John.

The knights are the religious military order the Pope recently charged with the care and defence of the Holy Land. This was now their headquarters. Richard sold the fortress to them after he took it off the Saracens and murdered its defenders when they surrendered.

"Some people," William explained to me, "are now naming the Knights of Saint John as the Hospitaller Knights because they provide hospices to shelter the pilgrims and guards for the pilgrim caravans."

******

Acre was quite impressive. Indeed, there were so many boats at the quay we had to wait in the harbour for hours until the wind changed and a cog could be pulled away from the quay to provide space for one of our galleys.

Harold solved the problem of mooring both galleys in one mooring position. He moored our galley to the quay in the cog's place, and then had our companion galley lash itself to us. It all took some time to accomplish, and I could see William getting more and more anxious as we waited.

I don't think William was anxious for any particular reason; he just wanted to get on with it.

As you might imagine, because it is the principal port for Jerusalem, even though Jerusalem is now in Saracen hands, the quay was quite busy with pilgrims and refugees coming and going and labourers and slaves trudging up and down the quay loading and unloading cargo boats.

******

A Hospitaller Knight wearing the order's black surcoat with a white cross stood silently watching while our galley finished mooring and the second galley came slowly alongside to be lashed to ours.

When we finished lashing the galleys together and mooring Harold's to the quay, the knight stepped forward and rather arrogantly demanded to know who we were and our purpose and intentions.

Lord William responded most respectfully and explained our purpose.

"Good morning, Sir Knight, I am William, Admiral of the English Fleet, and these are two of my galleys. We were bound from Cyprus to Latika to rescue stranded Christians and others fleeing the Saracens. As you may know, we have undertaken the task of carrying refugees to safety now that the Bekka Valley has fallen and the road to Beirut is open to the Saracens.

"Unfortunately, we rowed too far to the south last night so I decided to put in here for a few hours to obtain water and to see if we might be of service to the local pilgrims and merchants, with the permission of your illustrious order, of course.

"Also, whilst we are here, we'd like to see if there are any fighting men in the city who would join our company as sailors or men-at-arms serving at sea to help fight the Saracen pirates."

The knight's response surprised us.

"We've heard of your efforts and that you might be coming to Acre, Lord William. I was sent to welcome to you."

Then he surprised us again.

"We received word of the death of Lord Edmund and the loss of his fief from refugees coming down the coastal track. More have been arriving every day, more than we can possibly feed and shelter. It is most fortunate, and thus God's Will, that you are here to carry some of them to safety."

Hmm. I'm surprised. He knows William has been nobled and that we might be coming here? How does he know these things? Who are these knights?

******

Word travelled swiftly and within minutes of setting foot on the quay we were besieged with refugees wanting to buy passage to Cyprus, men seeking employment, and merchants seeking custom and transportation for their cargos and coins.

Hours later, William and I were finally able to walk into the city to meet with the merchants who had approached us with various interesting proposals. One of the proposals we heard was something new—an opportunity to make coin payments in other port cities for an Acre merchant. He'd lost his son fighting against the Saracens, he explained, and had no one he could trust to do it for him. To my surprise, William agreed.

As a result, I myself wrote and signed the parchment contract saying we would, immediately upon its presentation in Limassol, pay the bearer of the parchment eighty-eight gold bezant coins, or its equivalent in silver or copper coins. We agreed to pay the bezants in Limassol in exchange for our immediately receiving one hundred gold coins in Acre.

I think I understand what William is doing—we get our coins immediately and can spend them here or take them to Cyprus. It means we'll earn twelve coins for ourselves because we'll only have to pay eighty-eight coins whenever someone shows up with the parchment and demands them.

It was quite a smart thing for the Acre merchant to do—it means he would be able to spend eighty-eight gold bezant coins in Cyprus to buy olive oil and such without ever having to actually carry the coins to Cyprus and risk their loss to pirates; for us, it meant we'd earn twelve coins in exchange for guaranteeing he'd be able to spend eighty-eight.

Is that a good contract for us? I wasn't sure.

"Is that a good contract for us, Lord William?" I asked.

"Oh, I should think so, Yoram. War galleys like ours are rarely attacked by pirates—so we are not likely to lose the hundred coins if we carry them to Cyprus or anywhere else—and we can spend them or loan them out or do with them whatever we have a mind to do.

"All that matters is that we must have eighty-eight bezants in Cyprus for anyone who shows up with the parchment—and we certainly have them, don't we?"

******

Our visit to Acre was a great success. Many experienced fighting men were willing to make their marks to join us and many refugees were willing to pay for passage to Cyprus. It soon became apparent we would be sailing straight back to Cyprus without visiting Latika—and be much stronger and richer when we arrived.

At least, that's what seemed to be in the offing as we finished a long day of buying weapons, interviewing sailors and fighting men who wanted to serve with us, and selling passages to Cyprus to rich refugees.

******

The sun was going down and William and I were peacefully walking with Aaron and several of the local merchants and their men back to our galleys. It had been a good day, and we were contentedly munching on bread and cheese and carrying a heavy leather sack full of coins to add to those already on our galleys.

At least it was good day, until several knights wearing the black surcoats of the Order of Saint John walked up and informed us that William and I must accompany them to their fortress immediately. *Uh oh. What do they want?*

"Is there a problem Sir Knight?" William asked. "If so, perhaps I can fix it?" *Can I bribe you?*

"I have no idea, Lord Admiral. I am only a messenger sent to fetch you." *Lord?*

While William and the knights were talking, I quickly swallowed my mouthful of cheese and handed the sack of coins to Aaron.

"Please go to the harbour and wait for us on board the galley," I said quietly.

I didn't like the looks of this. But at least they didn't try to restrain us or take the coins. I wonder what this is all about.

William had seen me hand the sack to Aaron. He gave me a silent nod of approval as Aaron quickly walked away.

****** *William*

Yoram and I followed the knights into Acre's great fortress. It was even more imposing and forbidding once you walk into its twisting entrance tunnel and saw the succession of tunnel gates and the many murder holes in the tunnel's ceiling and walls.

The Hospitallers' would obviously be hard to defeat by a direct assault. If its defenders were not prepared, however, they could be starved into surrendering if a siege lasted long enough. That, of course, was exactly what our company of archers helped King Richard do to the three thousand Saracens who previously held it—before they surrendered when their food ran out and Richard murdered them. They were fools, the Saracens; they could have held the castle with less than two hundred men and their food would have lasted several years.

"Can you tell me, Sir Knight, who it is that we are to meet?" I asked most respectfully.

"Why the Grand Master of our order, of course, my lord Geoffroy de Donjon."

"We are honoured, Sir Knight. Uh, Sir Knight, your Grand Master is obviously a most important man and worthy of the greatest respect; how is it appropriate for me to greet him?"

"Why, with a respectful bow and an acknowledgement of his title of Grand Master, of course."

And that is what I did after Yoram and I walked through the great yard and up the stone stairs to a great meeting hall. Half a dozen or so Hospitaller Knights were standing in a group around a man sitting on a chair as if he were a king on a throne.

"I am William, Admiral of the English Fleet, Grand Master," I said to announce myself as I bowed deeply and spoke the words in Latin as my brother had long ago taught me. "How may I be of service to you, Grand Master?"

Somehow I got the sense that my speaking in Latin pleased the Grand Master who apparently is some kind of priest in addition to being a knight.

"I sent for you, Lord Admiral, because I heard you are buying weapons and recruiting men to fight the heathens."

I nodded my agreement as he continued.

"My brother knights and I are pleased to know of your efforts—even though the Third Crusade is coming to an inglorious end as we lose more and more of the Christian fiefs and castles. My brother knights and I, as you may know, are sworn to slow the Saracen rot eating away at the Holy Land. We are sworn to hold Acre until another crusade can be organised and we finally recapture Our Lord's city. It is God's Will."

It may or may not be God's Will, but it certainly explains why the local merchants report that the Hospitallers have been buying great supplies of olive oil and corn and were not sharing any of them with the refugees. They intend to avoid the fate of the fortress's previous defenders, the ones we helped Richard starve out.

As he spoke, the Grand Master looked at me intently, very intently indeed, as if to judge my response to what I was hearing.

"That is good news, Grand Master, for it is surely God's will that you succeed. My men and I will certainly do all we can to assist you and the members of your esteemed order." *If you pay us enough and don't betray us and kill us as you helped Richard do to the Saracens who surrendered this fortress.*

"They say you are an honest man and that you are carrying Christians and Jews to Cyprus without stealing from them or selling them as slaves, Lord Admiral. Can it be true?"

"I would pray everyone believes it to be true—because it is true, Grand Master. My men and I try to live by the words of Holy Bible and the Church."

Well, some of it is true; we do carry everybody who pays enough coins.

"In that case, my dear Lord Admiral, I have a proposal for you regarding the Saracen weapons we took from infidels when we captured this fortress."

****** *Yoram*

In the morning, William and I admitted to each other we'd spent most of the night thinking about the Grand Master's proposal and what it might mean, and not just because of the Saracen weapons we were to receive and the four Hospitaller Knights we were to carry to Cyprus.

I couldn't put my finger on it, and neither could William, but there was something about these knights we just didn't trust. I spent a lot of the night worrying about Lena and Aria also.

In any event, it was settled—the offer the Grand Master made to William was too good for him to refuse and William had accepted it on the spot. The Company of Archers agreed to buy all the old and rusty weapons captured from the three thousand Saracen warriors when the fortress surrendered.

It was probably a good thing William immediately agreed to buy the old weapons and professed to be quite pleased about doing so—the Hospitallers might have been insulted and killed or tortured us if he had not. They were known for doing that sort of thing, weren't they? On the other hand, William actually seemed pleased. *At the time I wondered why; later, I understood.*

In any event, a contract to buy them was quickly signed and the next morning our men and some of the Hospitallers began working by candlelight in the bowels of the fortress.

What we were doing was moving a huge hoard of metal arrowheads and other weapons and armour to our two galleys—everything that Richard and the Hospitallers took from the three thousand Saracens when they surrendered.

In the end, we didn't come close to taking everything on this trip. We couldn't. What we did take was everything Harold said we might be able to carry without overloading our two galleys; any more weight from additional weapons, Harold warned, and our galleys might founder if we encountered heavy seas.

One thing was certain if the look of pleased determination on William's face meant anything—we'd come back and keep coming back until we got it all.

Apparently the weapons and armour were gathered up when the Saracens surrendered and had been rusting and rotting in the damp bowls of the Acre Fortress ever since. Many of the Saracen bows and arrow shafts looked to be warped and unusable but, perhaps, we could at least scrape enough of the rust from the arrowheads and swords to use them to arm our men or trade them for something we needed.

What we'll do with all the rest I do not know.

To my great surprise, Harold said the Saracen weapons and metal would make something he called "good ballast" to replace the stones holding down the bottoms of our galleys' hulls.

Until Harold told us about, I didn't even know our galleys had stones under the rowers' seats in the lower bank of oars, or that the stones were used to hold the galleys down in the water so they wouldn't turn over.

In fact, I didn't really believe it until I saw the sailors rip off the rowers' footboards and pull the stones out of the foul water at the bottom of our galleys' hulls to make room for the weapons and metal.

Oh well, a few more days of rusting and rotting surely wouldn't make them much worse than they already were.

In exchange for the huge hoard of old weapons, William agreed to pay the Grand Master the very small sum of fifty bezants and to establish a yearly voyage with a heavily armed galley to carry Hospitallers between Rome and Acre during the sailing season.

He also agreed to always make our galleys available to carry the Grand Master's coins and messengers to and from wherever they sail.

What William didn't tell the Grand Master before he agreed to his proposal was something I knew—the coins we'd been collecting from the refugees and merchants had been so plentiful William had already decided to return next year and make Acre a regular port of call for our galleys—and perhaps even establish a post here in Acre until the Saracens came.

Chapter Eleven

"Hoy, Captain William; welcome home."

That was the smiling harbour wharfie's welcome shout to me as he caught the mooring line thrown to him by one of our sailors, and a mob of people began to assemble on Limassol's old stone quay to welcome us back.

It's good to be home even if isn't really home, and it's even better to be a lord with a title fully bought and paid for. Who would have thought it? And Thomas a bishop, even if his diocese is now in the hands of the Saracens? My mother would be speechless if she knew. I wonder if she does. I'll have to ask Thomas.

Our return to Cyprus with two galleys full of newly recruited fighting men and paying passengers created quite a stir when we came into the Limassol harbour a couple of hours after the sun rose in the morning to once again begin circling the earth to warm God's creatures.

The excitement of our arrival and the talk it caused increased when we began unloading the warped and rusty Saracen weapons—and it increased again when it became known one or more of our galleys would soon be going back for another load and more refugees.

Thomas must have seen us enter the harbour—for he was there with George when I climbed off the deck of Harold's galley and on to the quay. The first thing I did was give my son great hugs and swing him round and round while he shrieked with glee. Then I held him tight while Thomas brought me up to date on what had been happening while I was gone.

What followed was a familiar scene: our refugee passengers with coins hurried into the city to find food and lodging; our new recruits and the rest of our passengers, those who bought their way to safety and didn't have a clue as to what to do next, followed us around the city walls to our little citadel.

The four Hospitallers we'd carried quickly disappeared; and Aaron hurried into the city to report on the success of our trip—and tell the merchants to forget buying arrowheads and swords for us and concentrate on providing us with arrow shafts and bows, particularly longbows made of yew or oak.

Aaron was quite pleased when I informed him that, despite now having all the old weapons from Acre, we would keep our word and buy all the blades and arrowheads the merchants had already accumulated for us at our previously agreed prices.

Although, I have no idea what we will do with them now that we have so much old metal off the Saracens. Sell them?

******

Our return from Acre resulted in a frenzy of activity. The biggest immediate task was to send one of our galleys back to Acre as quickly as possible to pick up another load of refugees and fetch the rest of the rusty and deteriorating Saracen weapons. *We could always use more refugee coins and the old Saracen weapons were just too important to leave behind.*

The decision to send a galley back to Acre was significant. It meant one of our galleys would have to immediately sail for Acre and then come straight back so it could help convoy the cogs to Alexandria. And that, of course, required decisions from me as to who was to go to Acre and which galley was to be used.

I don't know who is going to end up going to Acre, but it isn't going to be me. I wanted to spend some time with my son. I wonder if there is any quiet stream or lake nearby where George and I can sit and talk and catch some fish for our evening meal? I'll have to ask Aaron.

******   *William*

Thomas and I spent that evening and the next morning catching up on events and talking things over in between George periodically falling asleep and my brother working with him on his sums and his archery lessons.

Yes, archery lessons—George was being taught to push out arrows using a small bow Thomas bought for him in the Limassol market. *George was a right smart little boy and remembered everything according to Thoma*s.

It didn't take long to make the decisions. Thomas and I quickly agreed the best galley to go to Acre was the one which remained behind to guard the cogs. It could leave immediately while the others were still being unloaded and replenished. But who should be in its crew and who should be the voyage's commander?

Those were not small questions. Thomas wanted to stay so he could begin speaking Latin to George and learning him his letters so he would be able to scribe and gobble in church talk; and I wanted to stay because George needed to know his father loved him. I'd been away from him too often as it was. We needed to send someone else to captain the return to Acre. But who?

The more we talked about our men, the more it became apparent that we had several hundred men in our company, and not a one of them except Thomas and I were capable of making all the many different decisions that might have to be made about fighting and trading.

We had men who can sergeant the archers and sailors, of course—but none who could also do the required negotiating with the merchants and the knights and the scribing and summing it required.

Thomas and I were not going, and we had no one such person to take our places. It meant we'd have to send a team of men. But who then was to be the sergeant captain of the voyage, and who should go with him as his sergeants and soldiers and clerks?

It took a while but we finally decided who should go. The galley we took off the Algerians, the one we'd left to guard the cogs, would return to Acre on the evening wind with Yoram as the voyage's sergeant captain, Raymond as the sergeant in charge of the galley's fighting men, and Harold as its pilot and the sergeant of its sailors. We take a minimal number of men and only return with passengers if there was still space available after all the old Saracen weapons were loaded.

The men who are going are our best men and sending them is the best we can do—since Yoram knew absolutely nothing about sailing or leading men in battle, and neither Raymond nor Harold could read and do sums or, so far as we know, had heads for negotiating agreements with merchants and such.

And Thomas and I both agreed that it was a damn good thing we didn't need to send a second galley to someplace else at the same time. We were woefully short of properly learnt and experienced men.

******

Once the decision was made about the sergeants, our next chore was to properly assign our men so that we could send the best mix of sailors and fighting men with Yoram and his two sergeants.

So we summoned the three men and gave them their new assignments and explained their chain of command. It was important they knew how we wanted them to relate to each other.

Then we asked them who among our men they would like to take with them.

We'd already decided they could take whomever of our men they wanted—except that all the English archers who will remain here as sergeants over the men who didn't go. The survivors of our company were the only dependable men we could trust to help us protect George and the coins.

******

Finding the right people is a bigger problem than I ever realised; that was the thought running through my mind as I stood on the pooping plank and squatted over our newly dug shite hole. It was out beyond the wall of dirt and logs that was slowly growing to enlarge the size of our citadel and increase its defences.

It was a walk out here to the shite hole and the men didn't like having to use it, but Thomas insisted on it being here and required everyone to use it on pain of being struck from our roll for refusing to follow an order. He said the Greek physician tending to Brian and Athol said sickness comes when people spent too much time close to piss and shite, or it gets into the water.

He also said that he'd heard the same thing from the Greek physician who'd passed through the Bekka last year. And most important of all for Thomas, he'd read something about it in the monastery's Roman scrolls. The old Roman army commanders, it seems, said the same thing.

Whether it's true or not didn't matter one whit; Thomas believed it and so we compromised—everyone had to come out here to shite in the hole and we had an earthen jar in the yard for the men to piss in instead of wherever they were standing when they felt the urge.

The jar then got carried out to the shite hole and emptied into it every day until we could find a leather tanner who wanted it. They were always on the lookout for piss, weren't they? *Hmm. Perhaps there is a tanner in Limassol.*

Our most valuable men, of course, were our English archers, even the new ones who had just made their marks. They were the most loyal and dependable of all our men, to say nothing of the fact they were all seasoned veterans and fierce fighters.

Beyond the English archers our most valuable men were the sailors and pilots, such as Harold, who also knew how to use weapons and the newly recruited archers with longbows and crossbows who also know how to use swords.

What we needed most of all, in addition to more longbow archers, were sailor sergeants and pilots who could also captain a voyage—which required that they be able to lead men in battle and also know how to read and scribe and do sums so they could negotiate with merchants and officials. We didn't have a single one.

Randolph and Yoram were good examples of our problem. Randolph was an able leader of fighting men and seemed to be learning to be a sailor—but he could not read or write, which meant he could not write contracts or send or receive written orders and messages without sharing them with others; Yoram was a good scrivener and could do his sums and read and gobble Latin, but he was neither an experienced sailor nor a leader of fighting men.

"Well," I said to my brother Thomas with a sigh when I came back from visiting the jar, "let's hope that they understand their chain of command and can work as a team."

What we did was understandable—we made Yoram up to a senior sergeant and put him over the other two with Randolph as his fighting sergeant and Harold as his sailing sergeant. Yoram knows how to sum and scribe and was smart enough to listen to his sergeants.

Chapter Twelve

Sergeant Yoram

Randolph and I quickly boarded our men that afternoon and watched Lord William and Bishop Thomas standing with little George on the quay waving farewell to us. I was listening to the beat of the rowers' drum and watching the oars on my galley flash in the setting sun as we rowed out of the harbour.

The town's idlers and some of our men who had just finished their work are with them on the quay watching us go. And so was dear little Aria and her mother.

They all raised their hands in acknowledgement when I waved farewell and my galley turned to point its bow towards the harbour exit.

This was the first time I'd ever been the sergeant captain of anything. I was excited and trying not to show it. But Lena was distressed at my leaving so soon after I returned from my last voyage and, truth be told, so was I; but Lena's distress at our being parted, I must admit, pleased me greatly.

******

We sailed shorthanded with only forty archers and other fighting men to do the rowing, one man for every oar instead of two; but they were all strong fighting men, except me, of course. We left with a favourable wind filling our leather sail. If it continued, and we rowed constantly, we'd make good time to Acre.

And it did continue and we did row almost constantly with the oars from the lower tier of rowing benches.

We reached Acre's wet and windy harbour in the early evening of the second day and immediately moored our galley at the city's great stone quay.

And, joy of joys, I got no new blisters because I was the senior sergeant on the galley. Harold told everyone it meant I didn't have to row since I was in command, just as William didn't have to row when he was on board.

The trip was uneventful except for the cogs and fishing boats which began fleeing as soon as they caught sight of us. And this time Harold's piloting was more successful—we first sighted the Holy Land at the mouth of the Litani River, which is fairly close to Acre.

Even better, there were no delays at the harbour quay when we reached Acre. To the contrary, there was plenty of space available and a knight from the great fortress quickly appeared to welcome us.

Randolph and I and a small working party from our crew were immediately taken to what remained of the captured Saracen weapons in the cellars of the great fortress.

We would have brought more men in to help retrieve them but apparently the knightly order in charge of the fortress had a rule strictly limiting how many non-members could be in the fortress at the same time.

"We are taking no chances."

That was the explanation of the affable English knight who met us and told us about his order's rule. His name was Alfred and he seemed a rather simple soul. His father was a minor lord with a manor somewhere on the River Cam.

"Unfortunately," Sir Alfred explained ruefully as we walked towards the entrance of the great fortress in the waning light as the sun moved past us, "I have three elder brothers so here I be fighting the heathens for Jesus. They cut off Christian heads, you know, and eat their own children. Horrible they are, aren't they?"

Could it be true? I'd never heard such a thing.

******

It may have still been somewhat light outside, but it was black as pitch *and a bit scary* down in the dungeons of the great fort. As a result, we had to work by the light of candle lanterns both day and night. But our men worked with a will and the knights even sent some of their religious brothers and servants down to help us.

By the time the sun came up the next morning, more, but not all, of the old Saracen armour and weapons were on the galley as ballast, and we were able to turn our attention to the rapidly gathering crowd of people who wanted to enlist in our company or buy passage to Cyprus. That's when I announced my first decision.

"There is such a weight of weapons remaining that we cannot take them all without becoming over balanced and sinking. So we will leave some for another galley, or perhaps even two, and load the refugees who will pay the most coins."

Some of the people who gathered were so anxious to leave Acre that they had pulled on our sleeves and called out to volunteer their services as we passed by carrying the old weapons. Indeed, many of them waited all night for us to finish loading the weapons so they could be first in line to apply to us in the morning.

Once again there were numerous refugees who wanted to buy or work their passage, and numerous men who claimed to be experienced sailors and fighting men and said they wanted to join our company.

We did pretty much what William and I did when we were here last time, but not exactly. This time, we had them form up into three groups before we talked to them.

All the English speakers were in the first group, even if they weren't fighting men and had no coins to buy passage. I don't know why, but William told me he thought he'd been making a mistake by leaving poor English folk behind because they couldn't pay enough. He said he felt guilty about it and told me to give them priority.

Fortunately, there weren't but a few of them seeking passage, just a handful of women whose husbands died crusading with King Richard and a couple of elderly servants who years ago had been brought out on the crusade by their lords. They wanted to go home to die since they no longer could be buried in Jerusalem. We boarded them all.

In the second group were about a dozen experienced men-at-arms willing to contract with us as mercenaries, including a couple of Genovese crossbowmen with fine bows and quivers full of good iron quarrels.

We only signed seven of the men who claimed to be swordsmen—the others turned away when they find out they'd have to make their marks for at least two years of service and be expected to learn English and become apprentice longbow archers. Happily, the two Genovese were among those willing to make their marks on our contract.

The rest of our space including the rear castle went to the refugees who offered to pay the most.

And, once again, there were many penniless refugees begging to be taken so they could escape the Saracens. Even so, their desperation was nowhere near the hysteria I'd seen at Latika when the Saracens were expected to arrive at any minute.

To this day I don't know why the people of Acre were less anxious. Perhaps because the Acre Fortress and the Knights of Saint John defending it looked so formidable and they thought they'd be able to find refuge in it if the Saracens came.

In any event, all went well and I was greatly relieved—in addition to the Saracen weapons and the eighteen newly recruited sailors and fighting men approved by Randolph and Harold, we rowed out of the harbour with five English-speaking refugees, seventy-two refugees as paying passengers, a corn sack full of coins, and four Knights of Saint John.

The four knights were the only passengers allowed to retain their shields and swords.

I wonder why the Knights of Saint John always travel in pairs? I must ask someone.

Chapter Thirteen

Captain William

Thomas and I got back to work as soon as Yoram's galley boarded the last of its men and cleared the Limassol harbour bound for Acre and the old Saracen weapons.

Thomas returned to putting the learning on George, and the first thing I did was to check on the progress of our apprentice archers and get myself up to date on our various construction projects.

******

All of our men, both the new apprentices and our experienced fighting men, trained with weapons part of every day and worked on improving our walls and compound the rest of the time. And, of course, every apprentice spent part of his training time being learnt to push a shaft from a longbow.

The apprentices couldn't spend all of their time practising archery even if we wanted them to—they didn't yet have the muscles needed to push out a longbow and we didn't have enough longbows.

The lack of good longbows was the biggest gap in our weapons supply. There were a number of old Saracen bows in the Acre shipment but all of them were much too short, to say nothing of the fact that they all looked to be warped and unusable from the years they spent in the Acre Fortress's damp dungeons.

In a nutshell, we needed more longbows and long-handled bladed pikes. And when we finally get enough of them, we'll have to train our newly recruited apprentice archers, and perhaps all of our sailors as well, in how to use them.

Why train everyone how to fight with bows and pikes, even the sailors? Because it made no sense to have our men standing around on a deck until they could use their swords. *Kill them before they get to you* is the archers' motto—and from what I've seen it certainly applies to battles at sea.

Arrows were less of a problem. We took a tremendous number from Acre. Many were warped but some of them looked like they might be re-fletched with new feathers and made usable. At least that was the plan.

To carry the plan out, Brian had set up an arrow works in a corner of the sleeping area. He'd been teaching some of the refugee women how to shape and fletch arrows from tree branches and goose feathers and tip them with the Saracen arrowheads from the arrows we could not rework.

Some of the women, Brian reported with a nod of satisfaction, were turning out to be unexpectedly good fletchers. They did it in exchange for food and shelter, just as their men did.

*****

Until the galleys returned with the old Saracen arrows and their rusty arrowheads, Brian and his women had been hampered by the lack of metal arrowheads and the absence of a smith to make them and fix them. Now we had so many arrowheads Brian wanted me to buy more wood for them to whittle into shafts and more feathers for them to fletch.

Brian and Athol stay in the arrow works all the time so the women fletchers can tend to them; they were the only archers from the survivors of our original one hundred and ninety-two who didn't sleep inside our little fortress when they were not on our galleys and cogs.

One of the first things Thomas and I did after our two galleys returned was to relocate the fletchers, the kitchen, the men's barracks, and the makeshift huts of the refugees and the freed slaves. It had to be done because the bailey inside the inner wall had become too small to properly accommodate everyone and all of our activities.

As a result, our archers and men-at-arms came to be barracked on the other side of the inner wall and the refugees and freed slaves even farther out beyond the outer wall we were starting to build to improve our defences.

******

Except for young George and Yoram's family, only the surviving original archers and a handful of our most dependable new sergeants such as Harold are allowed to stay inside the inner wall when the sun finished passing overhead and night fell. The gate through the curtain wall and the door into our citadel were barred to everyone else.

If it was not one thing, it was something else. What was missing, now that we had so much old Saracen metal, was a forge to heat it and smiths to beat it into shape. And more of the old metal would be coming if Yoram's voyage proved successful.

When we were in Acre, I had inquired among the new men on my galley for smiths and found not a one. But, wonder of wonders, a couple of days after we returned one of the archers ran across a smith among the French men-at-arms we'd recruited at Acre. He'd been on the other galley and hadn't understood my version of French when I asked if anyone was a smith.

In any event, our new smith hailed from a village near Calais and his name was Alan. According to Alan Smith, he'd left his forge and gone off on the crusade with King Guy and wished he hadn't; he said he'd be more than a little pleased to return to his trade.

Now if only we can find a forge and some smith's tools so we can find out if Alan Smith actually knows how to use them. And where should we put it?

******

When we finally begin convoying the cogs to Alexandria, the English archers and the rest of our most dependable men will once again stay behind in Limassol to protect George and our rapidly expanding quarters. Most of our men, however, would sail with me to Alexandria. We would return to Acre later for the rest of the Saracen metal.

I'd be taking all three galleys and both cogs and every one of them would sail with a full complement of sailors and fighting men—and thanks to the Saracen weapons, many of the crewmen would have both bows to shoot pirates at a distance and newly cleaned and sharpened swords if they had to close in and fight them man to man. We even had some of the long-handled bladed pikes Brian and his blacksmiths have begun making, although I wasn't sure how they would fare in a fight at sea.

We had enough men to use them because some of the new recruits had become sufficiently good archers and had been allowed to make their marks on our contract. They'd come too.

I spent my days watching the sergeants train and test the fighting abilities of our new men, making sure some minor but necessary modifications were made to the galleys and cogs, and training our sergeants as to how we wanted them and their men to respond in the event the galleys and cogs made contact with the Moorish pirates who seemed so plentiful off the coast of the Holy Land.

****** *William*

One morning, a couple of days after I got back from Acre, Thomas and a small party of our men climbed the hill to the castle behind the city to visit the King's governor.

We needed more fighting men, so Thomas was going up to the castle to inquire about contracting to use some of the governor's men for our voyage to Alexandria.

I didn't go with him. We talked about it and decided it was much too risky for both of us to be in the governor's castle at the same time—he might grab us for ransom or worse.

Thomas returned in the evening in time for supper with a smile on his face. He told me all about it at dinner—and just as he got started with his tale I picked up a pot by its hot handle and dropped it in surprise—and got some suet pudding on my tunic for my trouble.

It seemed the governor received Thomas in his rather filthy great hall and listened intently while Thomas explained that he was there to talk about temporarily contracting to use some of the governor's knights and men-at-arms for our coming voyage to Alexandria.

The presence of the governor's men, and particularly his knights, Thomas explained to him, would help to discourage pirates from attacking and help defeat them if they do.

If there was any fighting, the governor's knights and men-at-arms would join our men in fighting against the lightly armed pirates. They would all do so, as is customary at sea, under the orders of whoever was the sergeant captain of their galley or cog.

Similarly, they will all join our men in rowing, even the knights, whenever the sergeant captain ordered them to row.

The governor liked the idea of earning gold bezants and silver coins without risking his life or position. So after a lot of hemming and hawing he made his mark to provide us with the services of all five of his knights and twenty of his most experienced men-at-arms for a voyage to the port city of Alexander in Egypt.

His price for their services was eight gold bezants.

With the addition of the governor's men, we would be sailing to Alexandria with more than five hundred fighting men on board our cogs and galleys. We would be a fearsome force.

And best of all, if his best fighting men are with us the governor wouldn't be able to use them to attack our Limassol fortress while we are gone.

The governor's present and future intentions were a worry despite the agreement. He was too arrogant, and he seemed too stupid and inexperienced to be understand our ability to fight him. Worse, we didn't know if his arrogance was because he was weak and insecure and trying to put up a good front, or because he was a great warrior and knew it.

I would bet the former; but it would be a bad surprise to fight him and find out I was wrong.

In any event, just before Thomas left to visit the governor, I quietly took him aside and made much of suggesting that whilst he was explaining and negotiating, he might also want to look around to see how we might take the governor's castle if it ever came to a fight.

Who knows—someday we may want to kill the governor or rescue someone he is holding.

Chapter Fourteen

Captain William

Yoram and his galley returned this morning with more of the Saracen weapons and his rowing benches full of new fighting men and paying passengers. But we didn't immediately rush off to Alexandria. To the contrary, we spent a number of days waiting while the merchants finished loading the cogs we'd sold them—and then several more waiting for the weather to clear.

We were waiting for good weather and fair winds because we intended to get to Alexandria as quickly and safely as possible. That meant spending the least possible amount of time on the water where the pirates might find us and come after the cogs. We'd use our galleys to tow the cogs if the wind turned bad after we got underway.

It was a fine day and the winds were right when I ordered the sails raised and our little fleet headed out of the harbour bound for Alexandria. Thomas and my son were on the quay waving to me as I stood on the deck of the captured cog and waved back.

Yoram and Randolph were together once again on the cog we bought off the poxed captain; I was on this one with Harold from Lewes as our pilot and sergeant of the sailors. Aaron was sailing with me as the representative of the merchants.

****** *William*

We were three days out of Cyprus when, damn it all, there was a possibility we might have found what we are looking for—the lookout perched on the main mast of Yoram's cog across the way just shouted over to warn us of five or six galleys in the distance.

They could certainly see us if we could see them. We were either outnumbered and in serious trouble or in luck and looking at some serious prize monies.

Ten minutes later and we would know whether we are either in trouble or in luck—the six galleys heading towards us were almost certainly Moorish pirates and they were coming for our cogs and their cargos. It looked like we were almost certainly going to be in for a fight. Hopefully, it would go as we'd planned.

The governor's knights and I and some of our men-at-arms, particularly all us wearing chain mail and carrying regular shields, quickly hid ourselves in the castles at the front and back of each cog's deck.

All the rest of our fighting men rushed to hide in the cogs' holds or crawled into their assigned positions under the sails we'd placed next to the railings all along edge of the decks of both our cogs.

From a distance, the bulges created by our men hiding under the sails should, we hoped, look like deck cargos that were covered to protect them from the sun and rain.

Our sailors also armed themselves and prepared to do their part as we had repeatedly practised ever since we rowed out of Limassol—before they pulled the sails over themselves to hide, the sword-carrying sailors and archers on the cogs carefully coiled the lines with grappling hooks attached and placed them all along the edges of the deck on both sides of each of our cogs.

A lot of time had been spent on Cyprus to make sure all of our sailors and archers were trained to use swords and shields in order to participate in the fighting. We were about find out if it would be worthwhile to continue requiring such training and practise.

By the time the sailors on our two cogs hurriedly finished their preparations, the only men who remained on their decks were three or four sailors pretending to be running about looking for a way to escape—which was what the pirates usually saw when they closed in on a merchant's cog.

Our plan was simple—when the pirates got close enough, the men remaining on the cogs' decks, the most experienced swordsmen among our archers and sailors, would pretend to dive into the cogs' cargo holds to hide—and pick up the shields and swords waiting for them there just out of sight.

"If we've done this right," I once again said to Harold who was standing next to me as we watched the pirate galleys rapidly closing on us, "everything will look normal to the pirates and they'll grapple us and try to board."

I was talking too much and repeating myself. I must be nervous.

Our galleys were doing something similar, in that the galley shields normally hanging on the deck railings to mark them as war galleys have been hidden and there were only rowers at a few of the upper bank of oars and a few armed men standing on their decks.

What we were showing the pirates was what the pirate lookouts would expect to see if they were looking at cargo galleys or seriously understrength war galleys.

Only if one looked closely, which the pirates' lookouts obviously would not be able to do at this distance, would they be able to see that each of a dozen or more rowers on the benches of the three galleys' upper oar banks had a rope and grapple under his seat as well as either a bow or a sword and shield. A few had long pikes with bladed and hooked heads.

What the lookouts on the pirates' masts also couldn't see on each galley were the large numbers of archers and men-at-arms who were jammed in under the deck—where the slaves usually sit—and ready to rush up the stairs and enter the fight.

When the pirate galleys got a bit closer, our three apparently under-strength galleys, one after another, started backing their oars and turning away as if they intended to avoid a fight and were fleeing without trying to defend the cogs.

If our plan worked, the pirates would keep coming and board the cogs because they thought our outnumbered galleys did not intend to fight. And that was exactly what they did.

I was in the crew's castle at the rear of our cog and could see and hear everything. Randolph and Yoram were in the same place on our sister cog and undoubtedly doing what Harold and I are doing—watching the approaching pirates closely and shouting orders as loudly as possible to steady the men so they didn't reveal themselves too early.

Galleys sit much lower to the water than cogs, so I could only see the stubby masts of the pirate galleys once they got close alongside. They were going to board us from both sides simultaneously.

I was so excited I was almost shaking—and all I could do is try to steady the men and keep a close eye on the ugly heathen who had climbed the pirate galleys' masts to act as their lookouts.

"Steady.... Everyone stay under cover…They haven't reached us yet… Steady…Everyone hold their positions…Wait for it…Grapples ready…Steady…"

Everything happened at once, when the first two pirate galleys reached our cog almost simultaneously.

Suddenly, there were a series of loud clunks on both sides of our deck as the pirate galleys banged into us and their crews began throwing grappling irons and using them to pull their galleys up against the side of our cog.

The hull of the cog shuddered slightly as each of the galleys was pulled against it.

It didn't take long before the head of the first pirate appeared. He darted his head up to look and then, apparently satisfied with what he saw, began to climb over our deck railing to board us on the starboard side. Two more heads soon followed and repeated the process.

They were close enough.

"Grapples, now," I shouted with my biggest voice. "Grapples, now."

All along both sides of our cog, just as we'd practised repeatedly ever since we left Cyprus, our sailor and archer swordsmen threw back the spare sails they'd been hiding under and scrambled to the deck railing to toss their grappling lines.

Our archers and men-at-arms who'd been hiding with the grapple throwing swordsmen came out right behind them and a number of our men started pouring up out of the cargo hold.

I watched the beginning of the fight while I was looking out of the cracked-open castle door and holding my hand up behind me to keep the men behind me in the cabin from charging out to join it.

I was holding them in reserve as we had been planning and practicing for the past two days. Harold was in the smaller castle up front doing the same thing with a smaller number of men. He'd send his men out into the fight as soon as he saw me sending mine.

From where I was watching I could see the lookouts on the pirate masts and those of the pirates on our deck. The incredulous and dismayed expressions on their faces were a sight to see when they finally understood what was happening.

Some of the pirates actually succeeded in climbing on to our deck before they realised they'd been gulled into closing with us and ambushed. Most of them didn't get that far—it's hard to fight when you are trying to climb over a cog's hull railing while an experienced fighting man is stabbing at you with his sword or pike and archers are leaning over the rail shooting a steady stream of arrows at you and the men coming up behind you.

A few seconds later, I flung open the door of the deck castle where we were concealed and stood aside for the breastplate- and helmet-wearing knights and men-at-arms who had been hiding with me. They charged past me screaming their battle cries and crashed into the handful of pirate boarders who actually made it to our deck.

I wonder who the pirates are; they look like Arabs.

It seemed like the fight went on forever but, in fact, it was all over in seconds except for a few pirates who were still alive on the galley our grappling lines were holding against our starboard side; they escaped our archers' arrows by diving down the hatch into the lower tier of rowers with their cowering slaves—and promptly got strangled and, for one poor sod, literally torn to pieces by their slaves for their trouble. The remaining pirate galleys began pulling away a few seconds after we sprang our ambush.

Our own galleys arrived soon thereafter and also grappled and boarded the pirate galleys.

The fight was already over by the time our galley crews surged on to the decks of the two pirate galleys being held against our cog by all the grapples. Indeed, for a few seconds there were so many of our men on the decks of the two pirate galleys that several of our galleys' men were hit by friendly shots from the cog's overly excited archers.

Damn, it's hard to tell who is who—in the future we ought to give our men some kind of insignia or tunics so the archers don't make mistakes.

Things did not go nearly as well for the cog whose fighting men were commanded by Randolph. The lookouts on the masts of the pirate galleys going for his cog saw our ambush in time to warn them to turn away and avoid being taken.

One of them got so close before the desperate shouts of its lookout caused it to turn it away that some of Randolph's grapplers threw their grapples in an effort to catch it. They fell short.

******

It seemed that both of the pirate galleys we'd captured came from some place called Tunis on the African coast. At least that's what the galley slaves on their lower banks of oars were finally able to tell us—after we threw the dead and wounded pirates overboard and I ordered some of our sailors and fighting men to act as prize crews on our new galleys.

The pirates' slaves were a scraggly and sickly-looking group, and mostly black. But some were obviously Arabs, and there was even a fellow with blond hair gobbling away with a voice no one could understand.

We found about forty slaves on the lower rowing deck of each of the pirate galleys—and they became absolutely thrilled and started weeping and crying out loudly to us and each other when we began taking off their chains and they learnt they would be freed.

We would send them ashore as free men when we got to Alexandria except for those who wanted to stay with us and had skills we might be able to use. If necessary, some of our sailors and fighting men from our cogs would act as prize crews and take their places on the rowing benches when rowing was needed for the trip back to Cyprus.

I don't know what Aaron and the merchants will do to crew their cogs after we reach Alexandria. They own them and our contract is to do our best to get the cogs safely to Egypt and then take our men off them and leave. Perhaps some of the cogs' sailors will want to stay with them. If so, we'll let them go and keep those who want to stay with us.

"Aaron, what are your plans for the cogs and their crews after we reach Alexandria?"

Chapter Fifteen

William's decision.

We could clearly hear a Moslem muezzin calling the faithful to prayer as we silently slid into Alexandria's harbour. The wind was light and blowing outwards from the shore so we were using the galleys to tow in the cogs. Perhaps the wind being wrong was why there was so much space available on the quay and the smell of rot in the air was so terrible.

It was the first time I'd ever been here. Alexandria was obviously a big city, with a large harbour crammed full of all kinds of boats including some with strange designs.

Alexandria may have had a Moslem ruler, but it also had a diverse population including many Christians and Jews—and its merchants certainly traded with many places if the wide variety of boats in the harbour meant anything.

Yoram said he'd heard that more than twenty thousand people lived here; Harold disagreed with a friendly smile—he said he'd heard it was even bigger, more like fifty thousand.

Whatever the number, Alexandria was certainly bigger and more bustling than any city I'd ever seen, including London. *And it surely is much warmer and just as foul.*

******

The harbour's great stone quay was quite long and the winds were favourable for outbound sailing vessels. As a result, many of the spaces along the quay were available and we had no problem finding space for each of our galleys and the cogs they were pulling in against the wind.

A number of people and workers walked towards us and gawked as our cogs were being slowly towed up to the quay and the workers prepared to catch their mooring lines— including several men who seemed to get quite upset when they saw the two pirate galleys rowing in behind us as our prizes.

"Aaron, do you see those two men standing over there where Bob's sailors are mooring the second pirate galley, the ones who seem to be arguing with each other and waving their hands about? Do you know them?"

"No, Lord William, I do not. I've never seen them before. But they were merchants from the looks of them. Not Egyptians though; they're not dark enough, are they?"

"Well, they seem to be quite upset about our having taken the pirate galleys. I saw them pointing at them and gesturing angrily at each other a couple of minutes ago."

"If you would like, I'll try to find out who they are. I'll ask some of the local merchants who will be meeting us."

"Thank you. That would be good of you and I'd appreciate it. And would you also please ask them to help us find a barber to sew and bleed our wounded men."

*****

Aaron jumped down to the quay as soon as the cog banged up against it. He immediately walked over to a small group of merchants who had walked up and were standing in a group watching us as we began mooring. They were standing together further back on the far side of the quay.

From the smiles and greetings as Aaron approached them it would seem that they were friends and had come here to greet him. *Of course, they were probably the buyers for his cogs and their cargos.*

I watched as one of the merchants nodded and said something to one of the men who was attending them. The man promptly trotted off briskly down the quay towards the city gate.

Aaron must have also said something about the two men on the quay for all the merchants simultaneously turned and looked at them. Fortunately, the two men were too busy arguing to notice.

Then Aaron and his friends began walking towards the cog, all the while talking among themselves with big smiles and broad gestures. I jumped down to the quay to greet them as Yoram walked up from the other cog, which had just finished mooring further down the quay.

Aaron's introduction was formal and in French.

"May I present Lord William, Admiral of the English Navy and recent victor in battles with the Moorish pirates. That cog over there at the end of the quay, and those three galleys in front of it, are among his recent prizes," Aaron announced as he swept his hand grandly to point to each of our four prizes.

We all bowed at each other as Aaron rattled off a number of foreign sounding names I couldn't understand. Then he leaned forward towards me and semi-whispered so everyone around us could hear.

"My friends know those men. They are not Egyptians, but they are big men in Alexandria because they sell captured boats and cargo for the Tunisian pirates. They sell slaves too. They are Arabs, not Egyptians.

"My friends also say they are dangerous men. They think you must be careful while you are here if they are your enemies.

"Oh, and yes, my friends have already sent for physicians and barbers to tend to your wounded. They say the physicians are Greeks and quite competent."

******

Alexandria was indeed big and bustling and crowded. Yoram and I accompanied Aaron and his friends into the city to be their guests at a meal where the dishes kept coming and coming and we kept talking and talking.

The meal lasted for hours, and we sat on the floor and tried everything; it was all delicious, especially the lamb and fish.

When we had to excuse ourselves to relieve ourselves in the alley, our hosts insisted that we be accompanied by some of their tough-looking retainers who sat on the floor surrounding us and ate as we ate.

Our dinner companions also look like tough men and so did Aaron, come to think of it. I suppose one has to be if one is to be successful in these dangerous times, what with the rise of the Saracens and the Moorish pirates.

After exchanging the usual extended pleasantries, we primarily talked about how we might profit by working together to defeat the efforts of the pirates.

There were many possibilities, but they boiled down to either providing our galleys and men to convoy the merchants' cargo boats to certain ports or using our galleys to carry the merchants' messengers, correspondence, and money or parchment money orders to those ports.

As the evening wore on, and the wine flowed, the merchants increasingly tried to talk me into setting up a post in Alexandria similar to that which we had established on Cyprus and intended to establish elsewhere. They seemed to know all about our intentions. Perhaps Aaron told them.

Alternately, if our establishment of a post in Alexandria was not possible at this time, they made it clear that they'd like to contract with us to base one of our galleys here to be available to them if they needed it.

Do they really want it, as they have been telling us, to periodically carry important passengers and valuable cargos—or do they want it so they can use it to escape if there are local troubles?

"I will have to think about this. We can do either or both, of course, if you and your friends will pay enough."

They all leaned forward to hear my answer when Aaron's friend asked the key question.

"How much to station a galley here permanently for our exclusive use?"

I thought for a moment before I gave them an answer.

"Each galley stationed here with a crew of fifty sailors and fighting men for you to use as you see fit would cost you four hundred gold bezant coins or their equivalent for each year.

"It would then be available to carry you or anyone you designate to wherever you want to go whenever you want to travel."

Then I held my hand in a gesture of caution to indicate there was more.

"On top of that would be whatever it costs for a defensible place for the sailors and fighting men to live when they are not at sea and someplace where the galley can be pulled ashore and stored during the storm season."

It sounded like a lot, but paying our men and providing them with food and shelter would take half of it; the other half would merely cover the cost of replacing the galley and, of course, be our profit if the galley was not lost.

It was late and the streets were dark and getting chilly when we finally finished drinking and eating. A number of men provided by the merchants walked with us from the restaurant back to our galley.

"For your safety," Aaron explained. "My friends do not trust the Tunisians—a murderer can be hired in Alexandria for a handful of copper coins."

We passed numerous men and women talking quietly in doorways or cooking on small fires along the cobblestone street. Alexandria, it seemed, never slept. It was a lovely night in early May.

Aaron finally asked the big question as we approached the quay and my moored galley.

"Would you really do it? Contract a galley to the merchants and locate it here, I mean."

"I don't know about establishing a permanent base here such as we have at Cyprus, but the answer is yes for us making our marks on a parchment to provide a galley and the fighting men and sailors to crew it—if your friends pay us enough money and have an acceptable place where the crew and the galley can be berthed when they are not at sea."

Whoosh. I've had too much wine to think properly about it at the moment.

Aaron was visibly relieved.

"I'll talk to my friends and try to have some ideas for you by tomorrow afternoon when we meet again. In the name of God, please don't sail away until we have a chance to talk again."

*****

Randolph was waiting on the deck when I woke up the next morning in the captain's cabin of our first cog, the one we bought off the poxed captain in Latika.

He waited with a knowing smile on his face when I raised my hand for silence as I staggered past him to go to the net hanging out over the stern and shite in the harbour. *Ah. That's better.*

"Hoy, Randolph, what's up?"

"Hoy, William. I have some questions for you, don't I? Mainly, I need to know what to tell the men who've been showing up because they want to enlist or buy passages. And then there are the damn slaves we took off the pirates, and the barber the merchants sent to take care of the wounded wants to be paid."

"Ask Yoram for the money for the barber. But what about the slaves?"

"Well, they won't get off."

"What?"

"God's truth, William. Most of them don't want to go ashore. They were afraid the Moslem slavers here in Alexandria will grab them and put them right back in chains. Even the blond guy no one can understand."

"Shite. Well, that won't do. Did you feed them?"

"Yup. I know how you feel about slaves, so I feeded them up real good. The poor bastards were starving, weren't they?"

"Well keep feeding them all they can eat and tell them they can help us row to Cyprus if they want. We'll sort them out on the way there.

"Maybe we can use some of them if they want to make their marks to join us as sailors or apprentice archers. The rest can take off when we get back to Limassol or they can work for us on Cyprus for their food."

We can use them all somewhere. Thomas and I have already decided—when the outer wall is complete many months from now, we are going to start a third wall even further out, much further out, and perhaps even put some kind of a boatyard in it so the men can work at building galleys when they were not at sea.

"Look there. That's what I mean," Randolph explained as he pointed to the men gathering on the quay near our galleys.

They've obviously seen me and Randolph and are drifting towards us. Must be forty or fifty of them. They've got some women with them too. It's probably the usual combination of men looking for jobs, people wanting to buy passage, and merchants seeking opportunities.

"Well, go pound on the cabin wall and wake up Yoram and you two deal with them and the barber. He's probably as hung over as I am from last night, Yoram, I mean.

"We always need pilots and sailors; so get Harold to help you talk to the sailors, particularly anyone who might be useful as a pilot. Check out the slaves too; that's how we found Harold.

"You know what we want and the terms as well as anyone. Board any English gobblers you run across even if they can't pay and certainly sign up the experienced archers if you think they might be useful and are willing to make their marks and join us; also experienced soldiers, but only if they are willing to make their marks for two years as apprentice archers."

Oh, my head hurts. I may never drink wine again.

"Also, and even though we aren't going to leave for at least another day, and maybe even longer, tell Yoram to start selling passages to Cyprus. Tell him he can board up to fifty passengers for each galley, but only if they are willing to pay at least five gold bezants or the equivalent, and double that for a bed in one of the deck castles.

"Tell everyone else who wants to join us that they'll have to wait; but encourage them to stick around, particularly if they claim to be experienced sailors or pilots."

We are going to have room for at least three hundred passengers and recruits because of the two new galleys—maybe even a few more, if some of our sailor men on the cogs decide to make their marks with the new owners. Damn. I should have talked to the merchants about that.

******

I watched as Randolph walked down the deck and began pounding on the wall of the sergeants' castle at the other end. After a minute, Yoram poked his head out and said something, and tried to shut the door.

Randolph was having none of it. He held the door open with his shoulder and I could see him waving his hands about. He was obviously telling Yoram what I want them to do.

It was early and the sun was just beginning its daily move around the earth. And for some reason I was hungry even though my head hurt.

"Tonio, bring me a bread and some cheese," I shouted to the galley's cook.

About twenty minutes later, wearing a sword and munching on a piece of flatbread with some melted cheese on it, I stepped over the cog's railing and jumped down to the quay. It was already bustling with long lines of workers and horses pulling carts full of bales and jars to and from the transports moored along the long stone quay.

There were squawking seagulls everywhere and not much in the way of wind. It was, I thought, an altogether nice, sunny morning even if I did have an aching head from all of last night's wine.

I could see Yoram and Randolph a couple of hundred feet away to my right separating people into two or three groups on the other side of the line of carts. There was none of the anxiety and jostling I'd seen at Latika and Acre.

Suddenly a warning shout rang out behind me from the deck of the cog. I looked up to see several men walking rapidly through the line of workers and carts. They were coming towards me from different directions.

One of them had a knife in his hand and the other had his hand under his tunic. *Oh shite.*

I stiffened, and I was suddenly glad I was still wearing my shirt of chain mail from last night. Too bad I didn't think to carry my sword unsheathed or carry one of the galley's shields or strap on my wrist knives.

I desperately started trying to pull my sword from its scabbard. They were coming fast.

Before I could even finish drawing it, the two men stopped just short of me and begin backing up—as Harold vaulted over the cog's deck railing and jumped down next to me with a boarding pike he'd grabbed out of the rack on the deck.

Attacking a sleepy man with a hangover who doesn't have a sword in his hand and isn't paying attention is one thing; coming against someone who is alert and has a boarding pike in his hands is something else again.

Almost instantly both of the men spun away and started to run. The man on my left turned around and ran back between the lines of carts moving along the quay and quickly disappeared.

The man on the right, however, made a mistake. He started running towards the men talking to Randolph—and they'd all looked in my direction when they heard Harold's warning shout from the cog's deck. They'd seen the whole thing.

As the runner was going past the men around Randolph a quick thinking young man with a short red beard came out of the group of men and hit the runner with his lowered shoulder to knock him off his feet.

Several other of the men were right behind him and so was Randolph. They immediately pounced on the runner, and I could see blades flash as I finally got my sword out and Harold and I raced over to join the fight.

By the time we pushed our way through the gathering crowd Randolph and a couple of other men were kneeling next to the runner with their daggers at his throat and the young man who had knocked him down was holding a badly slashed arm with blood dripping through his fingers.

Initially some of the crowd scattered but it all happened so fast they mostly just stood there and gawked.

"What the hell was that all about?" asked Randolph as he looked up at us without taking his knife away from the man's throat.

"I don't know but as sure as God made apples I intend to find out. Put him on the galley over there so we can question him," I said as I pointed to one of our galleys moored along the quay.

"And be sure to sign up the men who got him. Take them with you to the galley."

"Are you hurt, William?" an anxious Yoram asked as he pushed his way through the crowd and a virtual army of hastily armed sailors and fighting men began pouring off our boats moored along the quay.

Coming to help shut the barn door after the oxen got out.

"Not a bit. Harold saved my arse when he shouted and jumped down with a boarding pike. And that man over there jumped in to help us and got wounded for his trouble."

I pointed to the bearded young man who had been slashed by the knife of my would-be assassin.

"He's bleeding and needs tending to. Get him on board the cog and send someone to fetch a barber to sew him up and bleed him. Distract him from the pain while he's waiting for the barber by helping him make his mark on our roll, if that's what he wants.

"And sign up the others who moved quickly to help. Randolph will point them out to you."

******

Aaron and several of my merchant drinking companions and their retainers from the night before came running up anxiously about five minutes later.

There wasn't much for them to see; the crowd was already dispersing and the would-be assassin had already been hauled off rather roughly and had disappeared into one of our galleys for questioning. None of the local authorities, if there were any, had shown up.

"We just heard. What happened? Are you all right?"

"I am fine. A couple of men tried to knife me but I got rescued just in time by one of my fast-thinking men. One of the murderers escaped, but we got lucky and captured the other one when he ran the wrong way—right into the hands of some of my men."

"Who sent them? Could it be those men who handle the pirates' business here, do you think?"

"Maybe. We'll know more when the man we caught finishes telling us who hired him. If it's them, they won't be selling pirate cargos and slaves much longer."

That's for damn sure; I'll put a hefty price on their throats if I can't cut them myself.

"I am sorry we didn't get here earlier so we could help. We were on our way here to give you more information before we get together later today. It seems there is a warehouse available right here on the quay.

"It's that one right over there," he said as he pointed to a low shed-like structure with mud walls.

"It used to be used by a merchant for storing cotton bales and olive oil, but he disappeared last year and never came back. Your men could live in it and anchor their galley right here in the harbour."

Hmm. Interesting. I need to think about this.

"Well, I am not ready to say yes. I haven't even had a chance to think about it and talk to my men. But I am interested in knowing more. Yes, I am."

******

After everything settled down and my would-be killer was being "readied" for questioning, I asked Randolph and Yoram to join me for something to eat in the cog's castle at the rear of the deck.

They arrived thinking I wanted to talk about the morning's excitement. I had something else in mind.

"Something's come up. The local merchants want us to leave one of our galleys here for a year to carry their messages, passengers, and light cargos.

"If we agree, we would also have to provide the captain and feed forty or fifty sailors and fighting men; they would provide the pilot, the rowers, and a place for the men to live when they are ashore—one of the warehouses right here on the quay."

"Blimey; that's a surprise," was Randolph's response.

It was the first time Randolph had heard about it; Yoram, of course, knew something like that might be in the wind from our discussion with the merchants last night.

"The merchants haven't said it in so many words, not yet at least," I explained to Randolph, "but I think what they really want is a way to escape with their families and men if there is serious disorder and fighting in Alexandria.

"It seems there is talk of the Moslems giving the local Christians and Jews the choice of either converting to worship Mohammed or getting their heads chopped off."

And if that happens maybe we can bring our galleys here and turn a pretty penny carrying refugees.

"If head chopping begins to happen," I said, "we might be able to bring more of our galleys here and fetch good coins carrying refugees to safety."

"You're certainly right about that," Yoram agreed. "There are a large number of people living here who aren't Moslems. Many of the merchants are Jews and Christians."

"But what if the trouble happens during the storm season, when the galley is likely to be pulled out of the water?" Randolph wanted to know.

And then he answered his own question after he took a slurp of the hot tea in his bowl.

The tea here is uncommonly good.

"We'd have to have it on rolling logs and ready to launch quickly no matter what the weather, that's for sure."

"And it would have to be loaded with water and food at all times and heavily guarded," Yoram added.

And then, as he confessed to me years later, Yoram had a terrible thought: Oh my God, the captain's going to do it. I don't want to stay here; I want to go back to Cyprus to care for Lena and Aria.

"Aye, that it would," grunted Randolph, "that it would."

"But could it be done? Could *you* do it, Randolph, for more coins?"

"Oh, aye. I s'pose I could," Randolph answered after he pulled on his beard and thought for a second.

Yoram is obviously relieved because I asked Randolph and he accepted. I wonder why? Of course, he girl and baby.

******

Yoram's concern about being left in Alexandria with Randolph was so obvious it gave us a fine opportunity to have a bit of the jolly teasing him.

"I could leave Yoram here with you to help," I suggested to Randolph with a wink and a twinkle in my eye.

"But somehow I think he's as anxious to get back to Cyprus as I am."

Randolph roared. And then Yoram nodded his head and we all started laughing.

We were still laughing and smiling as we went through the door and out on deck. A couple of the sailors saw our good spirits and smiled too.

"Well, lads," I finally said to my sergeants, "we'll know whether or not it will happen after we meet with the merchants this afternoon and see if they'll pay the necessary. Now, let's go see if the bastard who tried to stick me this morning is ready to talk."

He was ready indeed.

Before I released him from his agony with a knife in his ear, he told us he came from some place called Alamut in the mountains east of the Holy Land. He claimed to have been sent with a friend to Alexandria several years ago to work for the Tunisians.

And, most importantly, he told us where we could find the Tunisians. When he finished talking, we dropped him into the harbour to feed the fish and join the virgins he'd been babbling about.

Chapter Sixteen

Captain William

The meeting later in the afternoon with Aaron and the Alexandria merchants was quite serious once we finished the customary tea and snacks— *excellent sweet figs*—and small talk about everyone's families and health.

To a man, the merchants seemed quite relieved when I reconfirmed we might be willing provide a galley with an experienced fighting man as its captain if the price was right. The negotiations that followed went well even though they lasted for several hours.

The sun was just starting to go down when we all spat on our palms and shook hands.

It was settled. For three hundred and eighty Byzantine gold bezants per year from Constantinople we would provide one galley and forty sailors and men-at-arms for its crew. They would be available at all times and heavy with experienced fighting men, with the understanding its passengers would do most of the rowing.

In addition, the merchants would provide an empty warehouse near the quay as a place for the men to live and a space on the beach where we could haul the galley out of the water during the storm season—and logs that could be used as rollers if we needed to launch it in a hurry.

The merchants would also, each month, provide the galley's captain with two hundred silver coins that could be advanced to the men for spending on food and women and provide someone to work full time at the warehouse as the captain's clerk and scrivener. They would also, and this was important, provide a pilot who knew the waters where they might want the galley to sail.

At Yoram's excellent suggestion, we were going to prepay a number of different merchants to deliver food and supplies to Randolph's men and let it be well known that we were doing so and why. Why? It was rather simple—so there would be no coins left for Randolph to spend that might entice robbers and pirates.

That was not exactly the truth; we were also leaving my money belt for Randolph to wear with some gold bezants in it for emergencies and also depositing some bezants with one of the merchants so Randolph and his second, but not his clerk and scrivener, could access coins in an emergency.

Our big unanswered question was which of our men we should leave with Randolph and who should be his sergeants. Randolph knew something about what needs to be done because he'd come with me to the meeting with the merchants as the head of the guards who escorted me. And now he was so pleased with his new command and his big increase in pay I think he would have agreed to take anyone we suggested.

******

"Tonight we are going after the Tunisians who sent the two men to murderer me."

That's what I told my senior sergeants. After a pause, I added an explanation.

"I just wouldn't feel right if I let someone get away with trying to kill me." *Besides, you and the merchants wouldn't respect me if I didn't respond.*

We soon set our plans. Other than Yoram, Harold, and Randolph, only Aaron and one of his local merchant friends knew what we intended to do.

At Aaron's suggestion, I did not mention my plan to the other merchants. Only my senior sergeants and Aaron and his friend knew we were going to try to eliminate the Tunisians before we sailed back to Cyprus.

I've got to admit my retaliation was a bit impetuous. But I didn't want to get a reputation for being soft and ignoring legitimate grievances— and trying to kill me is a legitimate grievance.

After the meeting with the merchants where nothing was discussed except the galley contract, one of the merchants, a bearded man in Arab robes, accompanied Aaron and me as we walked back to the quay. I'd met the man before but couldn't remember his name.

"His name is Farouk Omar," Aaron prompted me in English when we were out of earshot. "He knows where the Tunisians live and he speaks French and Latin."

A Moslem?

I looked at Aaron quite intently, and he saw the question in my eyes.

"He's an Egyptian Christian, one of the Copts who have been in Egypt since the time of Jesus. He's a merchant and the pirates have taken several of his transports, including one captained by his second son—they killed his son and he wants revenge."

******

Summer was nearing and it was already quite hot during the day. No wonder Alexandria tended not to really come alive until the sun finished moving over the earth—and then, once it did, the city stayed alive and vibrant until the wee hours of the morning.

Many Alexandrians slept and worked on the roofs of their houses and buildings to catch the ocean breezes, and the city was packed with migrants and homeless people who slept and worked and did everything else on the city's narrow, winding streets and in its passage-ways and doorways.

The city being jammed full of people working and sleeping and living outside raised a major problem: how were we to take a force of heavily armed foreign sailors and men-at-arms through the city's crowded streets and alleys to where the Tunisians live without them being alerted to the fact we were coming?

Farouk was the answer. Aaron arranged for Farouk and a couple of his elderly retainers to guide us through the city.

The first thing I did was have the four Egyptians come aboard Harold's galley. Once aboard, Randolph and I questioned them at length about the location of the Tunisians and the size and nature of the compound in which they resided and conducted their business. Harold and Yoram listened intently as we did.

When we finished, Randolph and a couple of our steadiest men put on Egyptian robes and went with Farouk to spy out the Tunisians' home. According to Farouk, it was inside the city walls in the eastern part of the big city.

Another three of our men were sent by Randolph to keep an eye on the barracks of the city watch for the entire night. He didn't tell them why; just that we must be instantly informed any time a group of more than ten of the city watchmen left the barracks together.

Seeing Randolph in Egyptian robes gave me an idea. So after he went off to locate the Tunisians, I began organising our assault force and Yoram, who had already gone to the market once to buy Egyptian clothes for Randolph, went back to buy another sixty of the lightweight cotton robes and head scarves worn by most Egyptian men.

It is always better to take too many men to a fight than too few, so that was what I decided to do. I also decided it might be helpful if some of the men who came with us could speak French so they could understand Farouk.

So who among our fighting men who spoke French? Harold recalled one of his fellow galley slaves, a soldier who came from one of the Norman villages near Calais. He spoke French for sure, and was on one of the galleys.

According to Harold, the man's name was Henry and he was a very experienced soldier from Normandy who had fought in the crusades and been captured. He was likely to know others among our men who spoke French; so off went a runner to find Henry.

One thing we were almost certain to need is some kind of battering ram to knock down the Tunisians' gates and doors.

So after Yoram returned with the Egyptian robes he once again, with four or five men to guard him and the coins he is carrying, went to the wood yard district a few blocks past the end of the quay. It had all kinds of wood for sale from newly cut logs to the flat pieces used by carpenters and wrights. He used some copper coins to buy a tree trunk with the stubs of its branches still on it.

Yoram had the men carry the tree trunk back and drop it on the quay in front of our galley—and then he had them sit on it while we waited for our scouting party to return.

By the time Randolph and Farouk returned, I'd appointed Henry to be Randolph's chosen man for tonight's excursion, what the French call a corporal. Henry and I quickly put together a force of about fifty of our archers and men-at-arms "for guard duty tonight."

We assembled our "guard force" on one of the galleys. Then I had Harold move the galley away from the quay so no one could get off to leak the secret of where we were going and what we intended to do when we got there.

According to Henry, six or seven of the men he had selected spoke at least passable French. They'd be the guards for our elderly guides and translate for them.

All each of the men Henry and I selected to be a guard knew was that he was being temporarily seconded to a guard force charged with preventing our galleys and the merchants' cogs from being cut out and taken away as prizes.

Each of the "guards" was only told to bring a small galley shield and a sword and quietly report to one of our galleys moored at the quay for duty an hour after dark. Those who were archers were to bring their longbows and two quivers of arrows instead of a sword and shield.

******

Once the sun went down and all the men were aboard the galley, it was rowed out into the harbour from where it was moored and each of the men was given one of the white cotton robes and a head scarf and told to put them on.

There was a lot of quiet talk and more than a little excitement among the men as they waited on the galley deck in the dark. They had no idea what their "guard assignment" might be but it was clear to all of them something was up and they were going to be part of it.

Yoram and his guards waited on the quay for Randolph and his scouts. When they returned Yoram brought them out to us in a dinghy.

******

It was three or four hours after sundown when Randolph finally climbed aboard the darkened galley slowly swinging in response to the wind and the waves in the harbour. It was still early—the city and quay were still alive with activity and will undoubtedly remain so well into the night.

So far it looked like our raid on the Tunisians was good to go. One or another of the three men we had watching the compound and barracks of the men of the city watch returned every so often to report. According to the latest messenger, everything appeared normal.

Some of our men were keeping an eye on the city watch's compound from a wine shop opposite its entrance. The only problem, the latest messenger reported before he headed back, was the coins he was losing money gambling while he and the others drank wine and watched the comings and goings of the city's watchmen. The gambling was, he explained, a good excuse for them to be seated there.

We had a light moment and everyone laughed, including the messenger, when he asked if he would be reimbursed for his gambling losses since they were "in the line of duty."

Wine shop? I thought Moslems didn't drink.

"A wine shop, Aaron? I thought Alexandria was a Moslem city."

******

The night was more than half gone and the activity in the city's streets and along the quay was finally slowing down. That's when the men chosen for the raid hauled on the long line attaching the galley to the quay and quietly pulled it back into place against the quay so they could disembark.

I watched and listened as the men silently climbed over the galley rail and assembled on the nearly empty quay. Henry and his sergeants made sure there was no talking.

While we were anchored in the harbour, I'd explained to the men what we are going to do. They understood that our safety and the success of our raid meant they had to be quiet and not in any way talk or draw attention to themselves when they got off the galley and moved through the city's narrow streets and alleys.

At least, I hope I have made sure they will keep quiet; I even put a finger to my lips and said "shh" to each man as he climbed over the galley railing and joined the men following Randolph and the scouts. They may be good fighters and archers, but some of them don't speak any language I've ever heard before. Hopefully they understood "shh."

We did not walk directly to the walled compound of the Tunisians. To the contrary, because Aaron believed we were probably being watched, we all casually ambled down the quay in the opposite direction and then headed into the city along a densely packed narrow street heading away from where Farouk said we would find the Tunisians.

The men of the city watch were nowhere to be seen. *They were probably, I hope, off collecting protection money and carousing in the taverns as the merchants had explained when we first arrived.*

Farouk led our men through the narrow city lanes and alleys in a great round-about route to the compound where the Tunisians were thought to live. It was late, but there were still a surprisingly large number of people on the streets.

The flickering of candles in the workshops along the way suggested many of the city's artisans preferred working in the relative cool of the dimly lit night to working in the summertime heat of the day when they can see better. *Or more likely they work both day and night.*

There were far too many of us to be inconspicuous. In the moonlight and by the light of the flickering fires, we could see people openly looking at us with curious eyes as we walked along the narrow lanes.

Our behaviour was casual, and our swords and weapons were hidden as best they could be under our tan robes. But the people in the streets could obviously see the small boat shields and longbows we were carrying and knew we were heading somewhere with a purpose, and possibly a violent one. But they didn't know where or why. *At least I hope not.*

And, sure enough, we were followed.

One of Farouk's elderly retainers deliberately brought up the rear some distance behind our main group of men along with Henry and two other men Randolph had identified as possible sergeants. They soon spotted the man trailing along behind us—and took him when he followed us down a long and quiet alley, so narrow in places I could actually touch the mud walls on either side of it at the same time.

He had no chance of escape once the narrow alley was blocked at each end.

Our follower was quickly questioned. He initially claimed to be following us because he was curious; then, he claimed to be watching us for merchants whose names he could not remember; then, he admitted to be working for the Tunisians; and then he suffered a knife slash across his throat and died like a butchered ox.

At the end of the narrow alley, we turned a hard left and continued in the moonlight, despite everywhere drawing the intense observations of the people still in the streets and workshops and dozing in the doorways. We could hear people talking quietly, but no one called after us or seemed alarmed.

Ten minutes or so later, we took another hard left and Farouk and Randolph stepped up their pace as we unsheathed our swords, nocked arrows, and began trotting forward. That's when people on the street began to react.

Out of the corner of my eye, I could see them begin to whisper to each other and hurriedly pack up to leave the area. Those who could began to close and bar their doors and gates. Everyone left quickly. Within seconds, the entire neighbourhood through which we were passing looked and sounded deserted.

Not a single loud word was spoken by the people in the street. The only sounds were a few whispers as sleepers were shaken awake, the clunking as gates and doors were closed and barred, and the slapping of bare and sandaled feet moving away on the narrow cobblestone lane running in the front and sides of the Tunisians' compound.

Once we reached the entrance to the Tunisians' compound, we waited for about a minute to give our men time to move down the streets around the compound to surround it.

When it seemed as though everyone had had enough time to get in place, I waved my hand and nodded to Henry and the men carrying the log.

They could see my signal in the moonlight and needed only one big swing of the log to batter down the wooden door leading into the courtyard. Once inside the courtyard, they rushed to the door of the building in it and knocked it open as well.

The two men and their families were certainly awakened by the noise of the gate being battered down. But we moved so fast they barely had time to begin pulling on their sandals and tunics before the door to their room was hit—and then they were overwhelmed by the mass of heavily armed men who poured into their rooms.

Everything worked out rather well. The Tunisians hardly resisted at all; although, during the brief melee one of their wives stabbed a French-speaking man we'd recruited in Acre.

It happened while we were tying up the Tunisian men and getting ready to carry them out. We were going to take them back to the galleys and question them when we got to sea.

There was nothing we could do for the man who was stabbed. She got him in the throat and he bled out quickly. All we could do was wrap him in a rug and let a couple of his friends take turns carrying him back to his galley. We'd bury him at sea along with the two Tunisians when we finished questioning them. The woman who stabbed him had everyone's grudging respect and was left unharmed.

Chapter Seventeen

Captain William

We spent the entire morning after our raid on the pirates' agents, our last day in Alexandria, selecting men to stay with Randolph and then selecting other men to fill the gaps left by their departure.

Deciding who should stay in Alexandria with Randolph turned out not to be such an easy thing to do when we actually turned our thoughts to it. But we got it done, even though it took most of the next morning.

We began boarding our new recruits and passengers while we were still selecting the men who are to stay in Alexandria with Randolph. Word had obviously gotten around in the city about our intention to leave with all our galleys. Men had been coming every day seeking employment and a particularly large number showed up today. So did many additional people who wanted to buy passage to Cyprus.

Among the latter were a couple of English widows with young children who somehow escaped to Alexandria after their crusader husbands were killed. We could only take them and a few more additional recruits and passengers because we were leaving one of the galleys and sixty men with Randolph. Henry was promoted to take Randolph's place.

The English widows seem like saucy lasses. I wouldn't be at all surprised if they have new husbands lined up by the time we reach Cyprus.

******

We rowed out of the Alexandria harbour as the sun was going down. Then we used candle lanterns on the galley masts to stay together as we rowed straight through to Cyprus.

We were overfull of passengers and carrying several big sacks of coins, so we did not go via Acre or Latika as I had once thought might be possible. We were also carrying parchments with money orders and commercial orders from the Alexandria merchants.

It was an uneventful trip except for the cogs and fishing vessels we began to come upon as we neared Cyprus. They inevitably fled as we approached.

We encountered no pirate galleys even though we were prepared for the worst with each of our four galleys carrying some of our money and passengers. We spread them out, of course, in case one or more of our galleys were lost.

Our Tunisian prisoners were questioned during the trip, and then tipped over the side to feed the fish before we entered Limassol harbour. They provided us with some interesting information.

According to the Tunisians, the Moslem Caliph ruling North Africa and southern Spain controlled most of the pirate galleys operating in the waters between the Holy Land and Gibraltar and had done so for some years. The Caliph's galleys were rowed by slaves and their crews were mostly untrained Berber sailors and cutthroats carrying swords and knives.

They also told us that many of the owners of cogs and ships pay the Moors tribute in exchange for being left alone. The boats of owners who don't pay, and sometimes even those who do, are taken as prizes and their crews sold into slavery. It's apparently something that has been going on since long before the crusades started, and even before the Moors began fighting the Christians who were trying to reconquer Spain.

******

The weather was good the entire way so I had time to sit on the deck and think once we finished questioning the Tunisians. What I thought about was George and Thomas and the future of my little family and the company of archers.

I thought about them a lot and reached some conclusions. There was no question but that I had much to talk to Thomas about when we next got together. Only one thing was certain—it was amazing how many coins can be made with war galleys and cogs and how much power and recognition one acquires by using them wisely.

On the other hand, it was hard to see how Thomas and I could grow the company much larger, due to the lack of men who could scribe and sum sufficiently to be our port captains and the sergeant captains of our galleys.

Randolph in Alexandria was a good example—it was not easy doing business with the local merchants and their overlords if you could neither read nor scribe nor do sums and had to rely on the honesty of a clerk provided by your customers.

And to think that only a few months ago Thomas and I were worried about starving if the Bishop didn't pay us.

******

Our arrival in Limassol was most pleasing. Thomas and George saw us row into the harbour and hurried down to the quay to greet us. So did a goodly number of our men who had stayed behind on guard duty and many of Limassol's merchants and townspeople.

It was almost like a happy feast day in my old village when the crops came in—and ours certainly did. We'd left with three galleys and the two cogs we'd sold to the merchants; we'd returned with four galleys and more sailors, archers, and fighting men. *And not a one of them can do the reading and scribing and summing we'll need our senior sergeants to do if we are to stay here and grow.*

"Hello, young man. You're getting bigger and smarter every time I see you."

That's what I told my son as I picked him up and swung him around and held him tight. He smiled and hugged me back. I loved it.

"I can count numbers, Papa. Uncle Thomas showed us; and Isaac and I caught some frogs for Thomas Cook. Their legs jumped when he cooked them for us."

"Did they taste good?" *Yuck. Slimy frogs.*

"Yes. Just like chicken."

"Who's Isaac?" I asked my brother.

"He's a boy from the city," Thomas explained. "His father is one of the wood joiners. I am teaching him and a couple of other boys to speak Latin and scribe and sum along with George. Good lads they are and now George has three friends."

Then Thomas got quite serious.

"I see you've brought in two new galleys. How did you get them and what happened to the one we bought off the old captain, and where's Randolph?"

I lifted George up on my shoulders to be his "horsey" and gave my priestly brother a gentle version of the trip while we walked along the beach track towards our camp and stronghold. Tonight I'd tell him more.

Thomas understood I was leaving out some of the details because of George. He beamed and silently nodded his approval and then proceeded to tell me what had happened in Limassol during my absence—absolutely nothing of great significance.

There had been steady progress, however. The repairs to the original curtain wall were almost finished and the construction of the new outer wall to surround it had begun. Building the new wall, Thomas explained, would move at lot faster once some additional tree trunks finally arrive. A third outer wall was just a dream at this point.

Thomas said he's begun sending hired wagons to mine stones from an old ruined abbey about half a day to the north. He also reported that there'd been not a word from the governor; although, he did ride by one day to see the work and ask if anyone knew when his men would be back.

******

Thomas and I counted the Alexandria coins into our chests and talked and talked until late in the night. The repairs to our compound and the expansion of the inner wall were almost complete—except now that we had more men we'd almost certainly need to build even more barracks to shelter them and the women they would attract.

Much of what we talked about had to do with when we would leave for England—or should we go at all? And if we did go, where should we go and, most important of all, what should we do when we got there?

Thomas and I talked all night and settled on a course of action by the time we ate with George in the morning—we'd take all the available galleys and a good portion of the men and coins and go to England in time to get to Cornwall and give the sad news to Edmund's wife before winter began in England.

We wanted to get George safe and settled before the cold weather arrived in England. If we waited too long before we sailed, the seas would be too dangerous and we'd get to England too late to find a safe place to spend the winter. In the meantime, we'd spend the rest of the summer in Cyprus and continue to send our galleys back to the Holy Land ports to earn more coins.

We are going to need more men and coins, a whole lot more of both, to carry out our plan.

Our biggest all-new decision, however, was that we would try to set up some sort of boatyard here in Cyprus to repair our galleys and cogs, and possibly someday even build our own. It meant we'd need to recruit expert joiners and boat wrights from wherever we could find them, probably both here on Cyprus and in the Holy Land ports we'd visit.

Recruiting such men was important; it meant the sailors and men we left in Cyprus when we sailed for England could help repair our old galleys when they weren't training or working on improving our living quarters and defences. If there was one thing Thomas and I knew for sure, it was the need to keep our men busy all the time. We'd also try to capture more galleys from the Moslem pirates as prizes of war—but not too many, of course, because then we wouldn't be needed.

Deciding to sail for England before the storm season arrived was an important decision, one that would greatly affect us in the years ahead even though we didn't realise it at the time; it meant we would primarily try to grow and prosper in England by bringing in more coins from outside of England.

******

"Yoram, do you know of any cogs we might use to attract pirates?"

"Attract pirates?"

Chapter Eighteen

Harold Lewes

A strange flotilla set sail from Limassol ten days after we got back from Alexandria. It included all four of the galleys we had in Limassol and a leaky old cog under my command—Harold Lewes, an English sailor man what was rescued from the pirates by Captain William through the grace of God after my many prayers to Jesus.

It all started when Yoram and I rode horses to Larnaca last week and bought a cog off an elderly Syrian Christian. The old fellow wanted to retire on Cyprus and considered himself fortunate to have found buyers dumb enough to pay good money for his leaky old cog.

After we bought the Syrian's cog, Yoram rode back to Limassol to prepare our galleys and I stayed in Larnaca to recruit a crew and plant ideas in the minds of the pirates' local agents. I was pleased to stay—my arse had blisters from riding the damn horse.

****** *Harold*

"I don't know why sailors are afraid of pirates. God will protect us since we'll be carrying so many silver and gold coins from Limassol to Acre for the Hospitallers."

That's what I kept lamenting to sceptical listeners in all three of Larnaca's waterfront alehouses after Yoram left and I remained behind to recruit sailors willing to brave the pirates for a trip to Acre.

"The cog is old, I admit it, but its age will not be a problem since it will surely be protected by God because of the many good Christian works the Hospitallers will do with the chests of coins and gold we'll be carrying for them."

After two or three days of talking and buying drinks I was finally able to find a half a dozen witless men to be my new crew. I immediately set sail for Limassol in the old cog to pick up our cargo of coins and gold for the Hospitallers.

My battered old cog did not tie up at the quay when I reached Limassol, and my newly recruited crew, much to their dismay, was not allowed to go ashore to visit the local taverns and women. Instead, we took on water and supplies and chests full of rocks while my men and I waited quietly at anchor in the middle of the Limassol harbour.

We waited until our galleys boarded their crews and departed for Alexandria. At least, Alexandria was where the galley crews were told they were going—and they, of course, had bemoaned their fate every evening in the alehouses of Limassol for almost a week.

William came out in a dinghy and brought me up to date on the plan and gave me my final instructions a few hours after my new crew and I watched the galleys leave for Alexandria.

As soon as William rowed back to shore, my poorly crewed old cog quietly left the harbour. We were bound for Acre with our imaginary cargo of gold and silver coins for the Hospitallers at Acre to use to buy more siege supplies.

****** *Harold*

The galleys leaving the harbour before my old cog were dangerously overloaded with sailors and fighting men when they rowed out of the harbour. But they weren't overloaded for long. The men stopped rowing and waited for my old cog just over the horizon from Limassol.

When my old cog reached the galleys, they came along side and off loaded supplies and a huge crew of sailors and heavily armed archers and men-at-arms—almost two hundred and fifty fighting men and enough food and water for more than three weeks of sailing.

When my new crew and supplies were all aboard, I ordered the sails of my now greatly over-crewed cog hoisted and we set out in the general direction of Acre.

The galleys and their now-skeleton crews did not come with us. They split up and each headed for a different port on the coast of the Holy Land to gather coins by carrying refugees and parchments.

The galleys should do well. Their captains and sergeants had all been on at least two of our three previous refugee carrying voyages. They knew what to do.

Alan, an archer from Sheffield, was in charge of the galley bound for Latika; Yoram the one heading for Acre to pick up more of the Hospitallers' metal. Each of the other two galleys was under one of the archer sergeants; Henry's was bound for Tartus and Phillip's for Tripoli.

And where were Lord William and Bishop Thomas? Why, they were staying in Limassol with George and the rest of the archers and holding their breaths. So was everybody else who knew where the galleys were going and what the cog would be doing.

Surely most of them will get through to the Holy Land and be able to return with coins and refugees. But what will happen to me and my cog?

****** *Harold*

The first pirate galley appeared in the distance only a few hours after the galleys moved off towards the Holy Land with their skeleton crews. It was waiting for us and knew exactly where to find us. Its crew had obviously gotten word from their spies in Larnaca about our voyage from Limassol loaded with coins and gold for the Hospitaller Knights at Acre.

I quickly ordered the cog to do what pirates would expect it to do—turn to the south and run with the wind at its back in an effort to get away.

There was to be no escape. The pirate came alongside and its grapples thumped on to the cog's deck as my crew ran for the deck hatch in a desperate effort to escape by hiding in the cargo hold. At least, that was what it looked like to the pirates' lookout perched high on the galley's mast.

The thuds of the pirate grapples hitting the cog's deck resulted in me giving loudly shouted commands from where I was hiding in the rear crews' castle. I was in there with all the archers and sword- and shield-carrying swordsmen who could be jammed in with me.

All of a sudden, everything happened at once.

The sailors on the galley side of the cog came out from under the old sails where they'd been hiding and threw our grapples on to the pirate galley. They threw many more on to the pirate galley than the pirates threw on the cog.

Each of our sailors quickly secured his grappling line and scampered to the other side of the cog's deck to get out of the way.

At the same time, my archers and men-at-arms screamed their battle cries and came out from under the sails where they'd been hiding, poured out of the castles at each end of the cog's deck, and dashed up the slippery wooden steps from the old cog's cargo hold.

We fell on the totally surprised and heavily outnumbered pirates before they even had time to cut their own grappling lines, let alone begin to cut any of ours. It was over quickly.

Most of the pirates were downed by our archers before they could even begin to try to climb aboard the cog or cut the many grappling lines tying the two boats together.

Within seconds our men were climbing over the cog's railing and dropping down on to the deck of the pirates' galley to finish them off. Indeed, that's where our only fatality occurred. One of our men enthusiastically jumped over the cog's railing to board the pirate galley and landed in the water—and sank like a stone.

A few of the pirates made an effort to escape by running down the steps to hide among the slaves chained to the benches on their galley's lower rowing deck. They quickly dropped their swords and surrendered when our archers drew down on them. The slaves didn't even have time to kill them.

A big brass key was quickly recovered from the body of one of the slave overseers and the slaves unchained. As they were being released, I bellowed out in English and French, "Are any of you from King Richard's lands?"

A highly excited Frenchman began waving his arms and screaming in Occitan, a French dialect widely spoken in Normandy and England. He was the only slave who responded. The others looked to be Moors and black Africans.

Within minutes, the decks of the captured galley and the old cog were absolutely packed as the released slaves and the surviving pirates were brought on deck. The slaves were excited and shouting; the pirates morose and worried.

Then there were splashes and screams and hysterically pleading men as the pirates were tossed kicking and screaming into the sea.

"Prize crew into the galley and load food and water for two days." They would immediately leave us and row for Limassol; we'd continue to troll for pirates.

I thundered the order over my shoulder as I was peering into the lower deck and motioning for the newly released French-speaking slave to come up and join me.

"Where were they from?"

That's the question I asked the French slave with a gesture towards the last of the surviving pirates as he was being pushed at sword-point over the railing and into the sea.

"Tunis, that's where the bastards come from, Your Excellency, Tunis."

"And can you gobble the language of those slave fellas, the black'uns?"

"Aye, some of it. Had to learn it to eat, didn't I?"

"Well then, gobble at those black buggers and let them know they'll be free when we make the next port. From there, if they want, they can stay with the galley as passengers and help our prize crew row it to Cyprus.

"Tell them that when they get there they can work for us on Cyprus for their food or they can go off on their own. You, too—except you might want to sign on with us because we'll be going home to England before the summer ends and France is close."

I was more than a little pleased with how nicely our plan worked out. And there was even a bit more room on my crowded cog now that twenty of its crew were off for Cyprus with our prize and the liberated slaves.

Even so, we were still overloaded with men. But, by God, I had a happy crew, and that included me—the men would divide up two hundred silver coins for every galley we take; every sergeant and prize master would get a gold one; and I would get three, by God.

****** *Harold*

My lookouts saw several cogs in the distance during the next day, but they didn't see any more galleys until the following morning.

It was late in the morning when the hail came from one of the sailor men I'd sent up to the top of the mast. He reported three galleys passing from left to right in front of us. Almost immediately there was another shout from the lookout.

"They've seen us. They were coming about. Looks to be three of them."

"Battle stations," I roared at the top of my voice.

"Every man to his place. Battle stations. Hurry goddamn it. Hurry. Rudder men get the wind fair behind us."

I watched from the forecastle as we came about to once again run before the wind, and my grinning and cheerful men once again disappeared under the sails along the railing and into their hidey holes in the cargo hold and in the deck castles.

Within seconds the deck was empty and the lookout who'd seen them, a Portsmouth man who'd made his mark to join us in Latika, scrambled down to join the sailor men on the deck. They'd been told to once again act as if they were scared shitless and didn't know what to do.

I shouted out the lookout's report so all the men would know what we would face.

"There are only three of the bastards, lads; regular size with two banks of oars; maybe forty oars a side and half of them pulled by slaves."

I didn't know that for sure, of course, but their oars were usually pulled by slaves, weren't they?

Then as loud as I could shout I added a bit of explanation even though the men already knew it.

"What it means, lads, is that we'll outnumber the bastards at least two or three to one and surprise them as well. And remember, we want at least two of them to grapple us before we show ourselves.

"We'll fetch more prize money if we can catch more than one. That's why I am going to wait as long as possible to give the word—so don't nobody move until you hear me shout. Not even if some of the buggers are on our deck."

And besides, they'll undoubtedly try to board us from both sides the way they did off Acre—so I might as well make the men think it's my idea and part of my plan.

The men responded with a great cheer.

"Quiet now, lads, quiet," I roared. "We want to surprise the buggers don't we?

"Climb back up, Charlie," I ordered the Portsmouth man. "Give us a shout if you can see any more. But then come down right smartly."

Then I began to worry.

What if they know how we used the merchants' cog to take the two galleys off Alexandria? Then what will they do—lie off from us and shoot arrows? Maybe ram us? What if they send in one galley to see what happens? Should I let the first galley begin to board in order to give the second time to come alongside? My head was spinning.

A thought and a decision came to me out of the heavens— *thank you, Jesus* —just as the galleys got close enough for me to see that one of them, the one on our port side, seemed to be slightly closer than the other two.

The pirate galleys were still a good four or five miles off our port side when I called out the names of certain of the men and told them to stop hiding under the sails and come out to join the sailors on deck as part of a little group of defenders.

In a trice, there were about a dozen armed men along the deck railing on the port side. I even ran out on the deck and pushed them into place where I wanted them.

As the designated men hurriedly ran to their new places, I loudly reminded everyone, at least three times, that the first job of every man of every man carrying a sword and shield was to protect the grapple throwers and archers from boarders, and the first job of every archer on the deck was to put an arrow into the lookouts on the pirates' masts.

Hopefully, seeing what they think is our crew preparing to fight will cause one or both of the other two pirate galleys to come in with the first one. That way they'd be better able to overwhelm my little force.

At least that was my new plan to catch more than one of them, and, by God, it might be working.

It was working, by God! The lookout on the mast of the closest galley saw the line of men taking defensive positions along the deck railing and began waving his arms in some kind of signal to the other galleys.

I'll never know what messages and warnings the pirate lookout sent. There was no way to ask him after he dropped to his galley's deck with an arrow in his chest.

What happened next was inevitable. All three galleys tried to come alongside and board us at the same time. They seemed to know what they were doing for at the last moment their rowers shipped their oars so they wouldn't shear off when our hulls collided.

I waited as long possible. Finally, I couldn't control myself any longer and gave the shout that sprung our ambush. But it only worked partially even though there were already pirates on our deck from the portside galley—I'd shouted too soon and I knew it the moment I did.

My sailors did their part despite the confusion and fighting as the pirates readied themselves to climb on board. They came out from under the sails where they'd been hiding and threw their grapples—and grappled the first galley quite nicely. But they almost missed the second because it wasn't quite close enough when I gave the order. Only one of our grappling irons was thrown far enough to reach the second galley and hook it.

Fortunately, the one grapple was enough, despite the pandemonium and fighting along the railing where the pirates from the first galley still didn't understand their danger and were readying themselves to board us. The grapple throwers whose throws had missed rushed to help haul the second galley close enough so those who hadn't yet thrown were able to put more grapples on it before it could get away.

It all happened in an instant, and this time there were snaps and crackles as some of the pirate oars broke off as our men hauled the second galley closer and closer until it banged against the other side of our cog.

The pirates on the first galley were stunned and quickly overwhelmed when I finally gave a great shout and my men poured out on to the cog's deck to engage them. They were all almost quickly put down by the time our grapple men had the second galley pulled up to us and lashed tightly against our hull.

But the battle with the men of the second pirate galley turned out to be an entirely different pot of eels from the relatively easy time we had with the men of the first. The second galley appeared to be bigger and have more men on board and, much worse, its captain had enough time to get his men organised to meet our boarders as they jumped down on to his deck.

It turned into a vicious hand-to-hand fight with casualties on both sides. And I was in it because I got excited and did something really daft for a sailor man who is supposed to be giving orders to his men—I vaulted over the cog's rail to lead my boarders against the pirates—and immediately took a nasty sword slice in my leg because I didn't get my shield down fast enough as I landed on the pirate's deck.

I ended up just sitting there with my back against the pirate galley's deck railing watching as the rest of my boarders jumped down and poured past me and over me to get to the pirates who were still on their feet.

Once I raised my sword and lifted my shield when the close quarters fighting came near, but mainly I just sat there against the railing and tried to hold the slash in my leg closed to stop the bleeding.

It was really stupid of me to go in with our boarders—I am a fooking sailor man not a swordsman.

It was a loud and crazy close quarters melee, and it seemed to last forever with everyone screaming and shouting and people fighting everywhere with swords and pikes.

The pirates didn't give any quarter and neither did my men. And to make matters worse, much worse, the third pirate galley dashed in and lashed itself to the second—and its crew came running across the deck and joined the fight against our boarding party.

In the end it was our numbers, and particularly our archers, that made the difference. We lost some of our men, killed and wounded; the pirates lost all of theirs.

William was certainly right about the value of archers fighting on boats. I must remember to tell him how useful they are.

The only prisoners we took were a handful of pirates on the first galley. They tried to hide among the slaves on the lower bank of oars after we came out of hiding and surprised them. It didn't do them any good—they got tossed over the side along with the pirates' dead and wounded.

Perhaps killing all the pirates wasn't God's will—for that's when the wind and waves suddenly changed for the worst and we first saw the huge, black storm rushing towards us. I'd been a sailor all my life and never seen anything like it. It was as if the devil had somehow arrived to sink us.

I was holding my wound closed and loudly assigning new men and sergeants to the prize crews to replace those who had fallen even while my men were desperately hoisting me back on to the cog in the face of the on-coming storm. The men I told off to be prize crewmen rushed to the prizes and were mostly able to board them despite the increasingly choppy waters and the rapidly rising wind. They had no time to load water and supplies.

It was little wonder my prize crews didn't take time to load water and supplies—the men saw the approaching storm and even the least experienced landsman among them understood they needed to get their prizes moving if they were to have any hope of keeping the now-howling wind behind them and riding out the storm.

My prizes disappeared from sight almost instantly amidst the huge waves and howling wind. And for the next few desperate hours, I didn't have time to think of them. It was terrible—I watched helpless as our main mast snapped and several men were washed overboard by the great waves crashing down on us as we tried to run before the wind. It lasted for hours, and then there was a brief calm, and then it started again and seemed to be even worse.

During the brief calm, we managed to cut loose some of our ripped sails and relocate our wounded and injured men to the stern castle. And for the first time in many hours I had time to worry and think. What should I do now—return to Cyprus or continue to sail eastward in search of more pirates since I still had two prize crews available and a man can never have enough coins?

But I worried even so—will Captain William be angry and demote me if we don't continue and try to take more prizes? It was a foolish thing for me to do—worry, that is, for the great storm suddenly fell on us once again.

Chapter Nineteen

Captain William

There was a great shout when someone spotted the two galleys coming briskly into the harbour on the favourable winds left over from yesterday's big storm. The galley in front looked more than a little worse for wear with part of its deck railing broken off.

The damage was probably from yesterday's big storm. I wonder whose galley it is?

Thomas and I decided to gather up George and his two little friends and go down to the harbour to find out. The boys were delighted to take a break from learning Latin to go with us to the harbour. They skipped along with us shouting and pointing and throwing stones.

"I think they were ours, more prizes, by God," Thomas shouted as we reached the edge of the beach and began hurrying along the track towards the quay.

"I recognise Little Matthew. See, he's the tall one standing in the bow with the mooring line in his hands. He's one of the men who went out in the cog with Harold Lewes. They must be prizes. Counting the one that came in yesterday before the storm that's three for Harold already, by God."

"Well, I'll be poxed. I think you're right, Thomas. Come on, boys, let's go get the news."

A few minutes later, we were talking to Matthew and hearing the first of what promised to be many stories about the fierce battle between Harold's men in the cog and the three pirate galleys and the strange storm that hit them right after the battle.

"I wonder what caused the third galley to come to the aid of the first two even though they knew they were heading into an ambush?"

Thomas asked the question and Matthew Little and the men of his prize crew couldn't answer it.

And where's Harold and his other prize?

"Did any of you sight our cog or the other galley taken in the big battle after the storm hit? Are they coming in behind you?"

****** *William*

We waited all that day and most of the next for Harold's other prize to appear. It never did. What did limp into the harbour with a jury-rigged sail on what was left of its broken mast was Harold's storm-battered old cog.

One look at the cog as it came through the harbour entrance and everyone hurrying down to the quay to greet it instantly knew it was in serious trouble and its crew in desperate need of help.

There was no way to describe the cog except to say that it was a right proper mess and lucky to still be afloat. Its mast was broken off about ten feet above the deck and the captain's little castle in the bow had been crushed by a falling spar that was still there on top of it.

"Thomas Cook, fetch some flat bread and meat from the kitchen; Billy, you run and tell all the drovers to empty their wagons and gallop their horses down to the quay.

"That's our cog and, from the looks of it, it's going to have a lot of men on board who are wounded and injured. Tell the first drover you reach to bring water, some of Andrew Brewer's ale, and an amphora of wine.

"Everyone else follow me. Let's go, lads."

And with that, I joined the men who were already running towards the quay.

Harold's cog looked devastated as it banged up against the stone quay and a hundred willing hands reached for its mooring lines.

Harold himself was sitting on the deck giving orders; unable to stand because of his wounded leg. Other badly injured men were laid out all over the deck and more were being carried out of the castle in the stern as we arrived. The men looked absolutely exhausted.

I could hardly contain myself as I vaulted over the deck railing and rushed to Harold to shake his hand.

"You made it, Harold. You made it. Good on you. Welcome home."

****** *Sergeant Harold Lewes*

"You did exactly the right thing, Harold. It was a good decision; and, by God man, you and your men are rich."

That's what William said to me the next day as he counted twelve gold bezants into my hand and my smiling survivors lined up behind me to get their prize money. *And there was still a chance my fourth prize would show up and I'd get three more.*

Later that day Captain William did something I didn't understand at the time—after the funeral service that Bishop Thomas conducted for our dead, he and the Bishop began having meetings with me and each and every one of my prize masters and sergeants to talk about what we did and they did and what happened. They even asked us who among our men did well and deserved to be promoted. I was first.

The barber said I wasn't to walk and take a chance of ripping my leg open again so I was carried into the room on a blanket and carefully helped on to a stool so I wouldn't rip my slash open. *So far—thank you Jesus—it hasn't started to smell.*

Captain William and Bishop Thomas met with us each separately and, as I said, I was first. Afterwards, I stayed as the others came and went one at a time. Some of the sessions lasted but a few minutes; others for quite some time. It was altogether quite strange and, for a while, I even forgot to worry about my leg.

We sat around the wooden table in the citadel, and each of the men was given a wooden bowl of strong wine when he came in. Then he was congratulated for his prize money and asked to describe what he'd seen and what he and others had done.

Captain William and the Bishop had bowls too, but I noticed theirs rarely needed topping off even though they appeared to be constantly sipping when the men did.

That's when I started copying them and going easy, although, I certainly enjoyed the first bowl. It made things easier somehow.

It was all quite casual and friendly. Even so, some of the men were quite nervous at first. *Including me, that's for sure.* But, inevitably, everyone who came in got excited and was pleased to have a chance to tell his tale and give his opinions.

Captain William and the Bishop seemed to be particularly interested in hearing who among their men had done well and who had not.

I learnt a lot too—and identified several men I will want with me the next time I go to sea; and at least one stupid bugger I hope I never see again.

Chapter Twenty

Sergeant Yoram

My galley was able to reach the relative safety of the Acre harbour just before the big storm arrived. *Yoram, your luck is holding, I said to myself.* Our hard rowing and the winds thrown up by the big storm got us through the harbour entrance just in time. But then we had to spin around to face into the wind and keep rowing just to avoid being pushed by the gale force winds into the rocks of the jetty protecting the harbour and its quay.

Some of the other boats in the harbour were not so lucky. I stood on the deck of my galley and watched as several cogs and a strange-looking Arab boat with two masts dragged their anchors and smashed themselves to pieces against the quay and the stones of the jetty. We, at least, could row to hold our position.

Through the rain I could see their desperate crews trying to escape by jumping onto the rocks as their boats smashed into them. Only a few of them made it.

But they had to try and so will all of us if it comes to it.

Then darkness arrived and the storm's ever-shifting winds made the situation much worse. We couldn't see either the quay or the jetty of big stones enclosing most of the harbour— all we could do was row into the wind and pray we were holding in a good place. The men were tired but they understood the situation—and they called out to each other not to quit. I rowed too.

Twice we almost crashed into the quay or the harbour wall in the darkness. We were only saved when a lightning flash let us see them in time for our exhausted rowers to stop rowing on one side or the other to turn us. And that, of course, resulted in the galley being blown sideways.

And then it happened—the wind shifted and one of the cogs in the harbour came out of the darkness and driving rain to smash into our galley and break off a number of our oars rowing on the port side; we could no longer row to hold our position against the wind.

A quick-witted young Englishman saved us, one of the men we recruited on our first visit to Latika.

He was rowing on the starboard side of the lower tier of oars and knew what to do when the oars on the port side suddenly snapped and the oarsmen were thrown off their benches. He instantly began giving orders and the oarsmen instinctively obeyed him.

Basically he ordered most of the oarsmen on his side to bring their oars in through the oar ports and push them through the oar ports on the other side and "row like hell."

The oarsmen did what he told them and their efforts on the lower oar bank offset the continuing rowing on the other side by the rowers on the upper bank.

Then, while the rowers' drummer and the deck sergeants watched helplessly with their mouths open in dismay, he rushed up and down the three steps between the rowing decks giving orders to various rowers to pull more or less until both sides were again pulling equally and we regained control of our position.

I was on the deck watching in horror as we came around to point into the wind just in time to avoid smashing against the quay. There was no doubt about it; he saved us.

****** *Yoram*

Everything was quiet and serene as the sun came up bright and clear in the morning. You would not think anything of importance had happened at all last night if it weren't for the masts of two sunken cogs poking out of the water and all the wooden planks and bodies floating in the harbour and the roofless warehouses surrounding it.

And, of course, there were numerous townspeople standing around and pointing and talking to each other.

My men were absolutely exhausted as we edged up to the long stone quay and tossed our mooring lines to a couple of gaping harbour slaves. Most of our men were slumped down over their oars in exhaustion, too tired to even go for food and water.

"Who are you?" I finally had a chance to ask the young man.

"Anders, Sergeant Yoram. People call me Andy."

"Your accent is English, Andy. Who are your people?"

"I am from Putney Heath, Sergeant. That's a little village in Surrey. One of the Duke's holdings, you know. My father is Anders, the village smith."

"Well, Andy Anders's son, I saw what you did and I want to thank you for it. Your quick thinking saved us and we all know it. And so will Captain William when I next see him."

Who will undoubtedly reward him handsomely; and in the unlikely event the captain doesn't, I certainly will. Andy Anders' son's quick thinking surely saved us.

Then I thought about things for a moment.

"Go get something to eat, Andy Anders's son. The cook was able to skin the wet bark off some of his firewood and get the fire going under the cooking iron a couple of minutes ago.

"The bread is almost ready and the cheese in the cheese amphora stayed dry even though we lost everything else. Report to me in my castle in the bow when you're finished; I want you to accompany me when I go ashore in a couple of minutes. Bring a galley shield and a blade from the rack."

****** *Yoram*

A little after sunup Andy Anders's son and I weaved our way through the crowd of exhausted men eating on our galley's deck and went ashore to talk to the Acre merchants. I was exhausted after only one or two hours of sleep, but it was time to get the latest news about the Saracens and see what opportunities might be available for us here.

We didn't have to look far.

The city's merchants were easy to find—the market stalls in the lane running up from the quay were packed with merchants and their men making repairs and waving their hands as they talked excitedly with each other about the damage they and others had suffered or avoided.

My God; it's almost as if they enjoyed the storm for all the excitement it caused, and their survival from it.

Andy and I, along with a couple of steady men carry shields and swords, had no more than climbed over the galley's railing and gotten our feet on solid land when I recognised a couple of the merchants I had met the last time I was here.

They were standing in front of one of the harbour warehouses with a number of townspeople who were looking and pointing at the debris and bodies in the harbour.

We stared to walk towards them—and when we began heading in their direction, the merchants saw us and waved their hands in greetings which seemed quite cheery under the circumstances.

But then there was a great shout, "It's the English! they're back," and a mob of people began running towards us waving and crying out.

My heart skipped a beat; we were in serious trouble.

"Rally to the Captain," Andy shouted over his shoulder at the men eating and lounging on the galley's deck as he stepped in front of me and drew his sword. So did our two guards.

We were quickly surrounded by the crowd before any of the men on the galley's deck could reach us. But—*thank you Jesus*—the people were not hostile, only excited and desperate.

Some of them wanted employment but most of were Christians and Jewish refugees from Syria and Jerusalem seeking passage, any kind of passage, to get away from Acre.

The situation soon became clear as they grabbed at our clothes and shouted and pleaded. It seemed that in the past few weeks there had been another great Saracen victory by the heathen king they call Saladin. As a result, another great wave of refugees was pouring into coastal cities still held by the crusaders.

It's a sad situation. But lots of rich refugees are exactly what William sent me here to find.

I knew what to do from watching William and Thomas and so did the men who'd been with us on previous refugee rescuing voyages. They quickly helped the new men respond to my shouted orders.

"Sailors, archers, and fighting men seeking employment form a line over there; anyone with enough coins who wants to buy a passage to Cyprus and safety form a line by the man over there, the big one with the bread in his hand who is waving his cap."

All went well after that. The merchants sat patiently in the shade and waited while I finished signing up a couple of pilots, both of whom claimed to know these waters like the back of their hands, and the only two archers, both crossbowmen from France. They were the only archers from among the many fighting men who applied to join us and the only fighting men I accepted.

The men were mostly deserters running from a losing war; not the type of men we wanted.

After signing up the potential recruits, Andy and I went over to the other mob of people and collected coins and jewellery from those willing to pay enough for passage to

Cyprus—and listened to the desperate pleas and entreaties from those who did not have enough.

Andy Anders's son was a great help. He knew how to sum and he collected the refugees' coins in the same old leather sack I'd carried when I collected for Captain William in what now seemed like the distant past. We filled it to the brim.

When all that was finished and the crowd slowly began to disperse, I was finally able to spend some time with the merchants. I recognised some of them from my last visit. They'd waited for hours, so I was fairly sure they had something important to say. They did.

They came straight to the point as we walked together to a tea shop inside the city walls—they'd heard about Randolph setting up an escape galley to operate out of Alexandria; they wanted something similar for Acre.

Their request was unexpected. All I could do is tell them the final decision was not mine to make but that I had a good idea of what would be approved and what would not. I assured them I would bring anything we might negotiate to Captain William the next time I saw him—but I could not guarantee how he might react.

Actually I do; I think he'll like the idea. Whether he'll accept whatever I might work out with these fellows is another question entirely.

We talked of many things—about the Saracens; about where I might buy the food and water we needed for our return to Cyprus; and about where in Acre and the nearby coastal villages I might find experienced boat-wrights and joiners who could be employed to help us repair our galleys and cogs on Cyprus.

The merchants, however, kept coming back to their desire to make their marks to charter one of our galleys for their own use just as the merchants in Alexandria had done.

One of them, a tall beak-nosed Greek, informed me he'd received a letter from his brother who is a merchant in Alexandria. He said he had a good idea of what kind of place we would need for a galley and for its crew.

All the men sitting around the table nodded when he said that he would try to find something similar for us, either in Acre or in a smaller and quieter nearby coastal town where the local lord was weak and wouldn't interfere.

The others were emphatic and enthusiastic; they all loudly promised they'd help and they all nodded and made sounds of agreement when one of their number sadly explained why.

"Our situation here is more precarious than it appears. The city walls of Acre are weak and badly defended. There is no question, but the city will fall quickly when the Saracens attack.

"The Hospitallers' fortress, on the other hand, is incredibly strong and well supplied and defended. It has its own water well and enough men and food reserves to hold for years, many years – but it won't last long if the Grand Master lets common folk like us take refuge in it and eat up its food reserves."

He sighed and leaned towards me. *And so, I noticed, did the others as well.*

"We think it most likely the Hospitallers will shut the entrance tunnel and not let us into the fortress when the Saracens come. It means our families will almost certainly be slaughtered or sold into slavery.

"We could buy cogs and fishing boats and use them to try to escape, of course, and some of us have already done so. But, as you well know, the wind is fickle off the desert hereabouts and we may need to fight our way to safety—that means we need a galley with oars and experienced sailors and fighting men to carry us and pull our cogs and fishing boats out to sea so we can get away."

I nodded sympathetically and explained what would be required in addition to many coins.

"Having a post near the harbour or inside the Acre city walls might be better for attracting passengers and parchments to carry," I told the merchants.

"But even more important is having a safe place for our crew to live and a place on the beach where they can pull the galley out of the water during the storm season and practise with their weapons when they are not at sea."

I know all that because I was with William in both Limassol and Alexandria when he negotiated with the local merchants.

Such places would be difficult to find in Acre, the merchants all agreed, particularly if they have to be near each other and close to the water. But such places did exist, they said, and they promised to find them for us if we would contract to station a galley here for them to use if the need arises.

"If need be," one of them announced pompously, "I'll provide my warehouse." The others rolled their eyes. *I wonder what that's all about.*

"We know what the merchants of Alexandria are paying to have a galley standing by with a captain and forty sailors and men-at-arms," another merchant says.

"Please tell the Lord Admiral we are willing to pay as much and provide comparable facilities."

I had a lot to think about as Andy and I walked back to the galley surrounded by a dozen or more of our archers and sword-carrying men-at-arms and an equal amount of merchants and their armed retainers.

****** *Yoram*

As soon as the sun came up the next morning, I sent a messenger to the stall of the corn merchant who seemed to be the leader of the merchants and asked for a meeting.

We met two hours later. Angelo and Andy came with me and once again I brought half a dozen archers and men-at-arms as guards.

"I've thought a great deal about what you have suggested and, although I cannot be sure, I think Captain William will agree. So here is what I propose— you deposit two hundred bezant or Damascus gold coins with me so I can show them to

Lord William to prove you are serious and will have a suitable place for the galley and its crew when they arrive.

"In return, I will give you a parchment its bearer can use to get that same amount of coins from the English Company in Cyprus if no galley comes—but if our galley does come, and there is no place nearby for the galley to be pulled ashore and no suitable place for its crew, we'll keep the coins and go away; if it stays, you give us four hundred more of the same coins for a total of six hundred per year."

Two hours of shouts, sighs, arm waving, and all the other things that make up a successful negotiation later, we all spit on the palms of our hands and shook on the deal—and I began writing it out on one of the parchments I'd brought with me. Andy had watched and listened carefully and silently throughout the entire process.

We agreed, subject to Captain William's approval, on one hundred and eighty Damascus gold coins now and three hundred and twenty when the galley arrived with thirty-five or more experienced sailors and fighting men.

It's more coins than William got for the Alexandria galley but Acre is more dangerous and we'll have to return them if a galley does not come.

Then I hurried back to the mooring space on the quay where my galley was tied. Angelo, the elderly Maltese pilot who was the sergeant captain of the galley at the time, thought we might have enough room to squeeze another sixty recruits and passengers on board.

I wanted to sign them up and leave for Cyprus as soon as possible, hopefully before the sun finished passing overhead, if we had enough water and supplies aboard.

Angelo was a strange fellow. I swear he walked and stared like a cat I once saw in my teacher's house in Damascus.

Chapter Twenty-one

Captain William

Yoram and Angelo returned today in triumph. With their galley safely in the harbour, it meant all four of our galleys which set out with Harold's cog last month had returned from successful voyages to the Holy Land. Equally important— every one of them returned loaded with recruits, passengers, and coins.

Yoram was particularly successful because he also brought back another splendid opportunity. But should we take it up or not? It was time to start thinking about George's future and make some decisions.

"Well, Thomas, what should we do?"

That was the question I asked my somewhat priestly brother as we sat around the wooden table in the moonlight quaffing bowls of Andrew's latest brew. I asked it quietly for George was curled up in my lap and fast asleep.

We were deep into summer and, as you might imagine, we were braving the flies and spending a lot of time sitting outside in the shade because of the summer heat.

"Acre, for sure," was Thomas's response. "Yoram negotiated a good contract with the merchants, he surely did."

Then, with a sly smile and a playful nudge of his finger to my chest, he added, "Better even than the one you negotiated for the galley Randolph is sergeanting for us in Alexandria."

"Aye, you're right about Yoram and there's no denying it. He's a good man, one of our very best. And the coins he picked up in Acre are more than enough to make it worthwhile—we'll come out well ahead even if we lose the galley before we collect the rest of the money."

"It's not just the additional money, William. He got the Acre merchants to agree to take a galley with only thirty-five fighting men and sailors instead the forty you have in Alexandria with Randolph."

He grinned at me as he said it. Then he added a thoughtful explanation.

"They paid more because with only thirty-five of our men there will be more places for the merchants' families if the Saracens come and they have to run for it."

"So, which galley should we send and who should we send with it?" I asked.

"Well," my priestly brother responded with a burp and a chuckle, "if he keeps brewing ale as bad as the swill we are drinking, we ought to send Andrew the Brewer and hope the galley sinks."

"Ah, away with yourself," I replied with a snort through my nose.

"Andrew Brewer will do better, a whole lot better, when he can buy the proper corn and such in England, won't he? But seriously now, Thomas, who do you think we should send to Acre?"

"Well, not Yoram, that's for sure. I certainly agree with you about him. Cyprus is much more important to us than Acre, and he's the best man to be the sergeant here when we are not around. On the other hand, perhaps we should stay here for a while longer, maybe even until next year, eh?"

Then, after a pause to take another sip, and grimace as he swallowed his ale, Thomas continued.

"We are running out of archers and most of them want to go home. But Henry might be willing to take command of the Acre galley with Angelo as his pilot and that young Anderson lad, the one Yoram says is so quick in his head, as his chosen man, or even better, as a second sergeant."

"You're right," I said. "It might work. Angelo and Andy already know about the contract; devil's bells, they were with Yoram when he negotiated it."

"Good minds think alike, oh younger brother. Those are the three I was thinking of myself."

"But if we do send them, Thomas, we'll want to select their men carefully and we'll have to find someone who can scribe and sum to go with them. Acre's far away and we don't want to send troublemakers who'll spend their idle time conspiring to take over or run off without the merchants and their families if the Saracens come."

After a moment to think a bit more, I added something we both had agreed would be important to our future as the owners of cogs and galleys operating in these waters.

"If we commit to the Acre merchants or anyone else, we must do our utmost to honour our commitment if we are to continue to earn coins in the ports." *That's for damn sure; it would quickly get around to all the ports and merchants if we didn't.*

"That's for damn sure but it may be harder to do than it sounds, William. We don't know the new men well enough to be sure we're sending the right men. But you're right about sending a galley to Acre. It's too good an opportunity to pass up. We'll just have to do the best we can with the men we have."

"Well then, which galley should we send?"

"That's easy—whichever one of ours Harold says will do the worst in heavy weather. We've a long way to go to reach England and the sailors all say the seas get much rougher past Gibraltar. I can't remember myself because I was too seasick at the time, but it's likely what the sailors say is true. It's also why George must go to England on whichever galley looks to be the safest; probably the second one Harold took off the pirate chief, the big one."

"And the old cog, oh priestly one; what about the old cog?"

"I think we should leave it here and have Yoram sell it; or maybe the boat wrights and wood workers can repair it so we can use it as pirate bait again next summer."

Then, after a pause while we both took sips from our bowls of ale, Thomas made a suggestion.

"Why don't we just go along with whatever the boat wrights suggest?"

Which will almost certainly be to repair the cog since that will give them more work.

"Aye, but it will surely mean repairing the cog if repairing it is what gives them the most work."

With the simple decisions out of the way, we got down to talking about the most difficult one of all: should we load up and start for England in a few days, or should we stay a bit longer and have our galleys make another run or two to the Holy Land ports?

And even more important, should we take George to England or should we stay here with him over the winter? And, of course, what we both have long agreed is the biggest question of all and the one we always turn to – what is to be George's future and how do we help him get to it?

"If George stays, I stay," my brother Thomas said emphatically.

"He needs to learn his letters and sums and I am going to be with him to make sure it happens."

Then we talked and talked and talked until, after many more sips and refilled bowls and an endless number of trips to the piss pot, we were of a single mind—*and quite tipsy.*

It was half way to dawn when I finally carried George along the path between the string beds of the sleeping and snoring archers and up the ladder to his bed in the loft.

Then I had to piss again so badly I barely made it back to the pissing jar.

******

Things fell into place in the morning and changed more than a little at the same time—Henry passed on the opportunity to be the captain at Acre. He was anxious to return to England with us and had another role in mind for himself.

"I am a soldier and a good one and I want to stay a soldier because it's what I do best. Even if the company keeps its galleys, the new men will still need to be learnt how to fight on land—and I am just the man to put the learning on them."

Henry was right, and Thomas and I knew it as soon as he said the words. We ended up making Henry the company's senior sergeant in charge of land fighting and sending Simon to Acre with Angelo and young Anderson as his sergeants.

Andy and Angelo were there when Yoram negotiated with the Acre merchants; they'll be able to help Simon do what needs to be done.

Surprisingly, not all of the original archers wanted to go back to England.

"Ah've got yon fletchers to watch over, William, and I want to make sure poor Athol is treated proper. He's coming around a bit even though the barber's given up and stopped bleeding him."

Yoram, on the other hand, was extremely pleased, ecstatic I'd say, to be able to stay here in Cyprus as our sergeant in charge of Cyprus and our boats and posts in the Holy Land; and then, to everyone's surprise, Henry changed his mind. He now wanted to stay here with Yoram to make sure our newly recruited archers and apprentice archers kept training and working.

There is, Yoram explained to me after Henry told us he had changed his mind and wanted to stay on Cyprus after all, a lass in one of the refugee families who has caught Henry's eye.

The big decision I made, and announced to my priestly brother and then to everyone else, was that George and Thomas and I would be leaving for England early in August and many of the available galleys and most of the men would be coming with us. Also coming with us, even though I certainly didn't announce it, would be almost all the coins, so we could buy a proper place for ourselves and our men.

Actually, we are only going to take some of the coins; we are going to hide a goodly number under the stones in the floor of our little citadel in case we lose the chests we take with us.

Our first stop would be Cornwall to tell Lord Edmund's wife he had fallen, and then we'd continue on to find a defensible home for George and our men. We weren't sure where we'd go after Cornwall although we did briefly consider taking George and the men to Kent where we were birthed.

We finally decided against Kent because we planned to continue using our galleys in the waters off the Holy Land—it's even further from Cyprus than Cornwall and the channel waters they'd have to travel are far too dangerous.

Truth be told, there was a second reason for not going to Kent, although neither Thomas nor I said it out loud—it held too many bad memories for both of us; growing up a serf in Kent was not a happy experience and neither was Thomas's life in the monastery good.

In the end, the more we searched our map and talked about it, the better Cornwall looked as the best place for George to be learnt and protected while he grew to manhood.

******

We were not going to England until early in August or thereabouts—and maybe even later than that. It meant our galleys would have enough time before we sailed for England to make two or three more trips to the Holy Land, and maybe even four.

"Why are we taking all the galleys to England instead of leaving some of them here to make more coins off the refugees?"

That's the question Thomas asked me when I announced my decision.

"There are two reasons we are going to take them all," I answered.

"One is that we want to arrive in England with as many fighting men as possible so that we can acquire a strong place to camp before winter arrives. The other is that I've decided to make a couple of stops along the way – to visit our friends at Algiers and Tunis."

"Not with George, you won't," Thomas shouted at me with a real flash of anger in his eyes.

"I won't have you risking him for a few more Moorish prizes. Never."

"Of course not," I hurried to assure my priestly brother.

"He'll be in the safest galley and far away—he'll be *with you* and safe in a Christian port while the men and I are visiting the pirates."

I emphasised the "with you." Then I told him my plan.

Chapter Twenty-two

Captain William

Things are moving right along. We now have a battered old cog, a headquarters fort on Cyprus, a fortune in gold and silver coins, and eight galleys, if we included the one with Randolph in Alexandria and the galley Angelo will pilot to Acre.

It appeared the fourth galley Harold took as a prize was gone—lost in the storm. It was the one on which Quick Ralph was on board as its prize master. With Quick gone and Randolph in Alexandria, we were down to sixteen of the original archers including me and Brian and Athol.

And soon there would only be fifteen—tomorrow one of our galleys was going to Acre with Simon in command and thirty-five of our fighting men and sailors. Andy Anderson was to be his sergeant; Angelo his pilot.

Simon wasn't the swiftest of our archers but he was steady and did what he was told; he'd keep the men busy and trained up, and he'd do his best if push comes to shove and the merchants and their families wanted to be evacuated.

Where they would go if the merchants decided to leave would be up to the merchants. Cyprus might be best and I decided to mention it to Simon before we sailed.

Simon in Acre, Randolph in Alexandria, and Henry, Brian, and Athol staying in Cyprus meant I'd be taking only eleven of the original one hundred and ninety-two archers back to England with me—and we were not even close to getting there.

****** Thomas

Being a priest as well as an archer and putting learning on George kept me busy. July passed quickly as our galleys shuttled back and forth to the Holy Land and brought back ever more coins and recruits and refugees with them. William was certainly pleased with how things were going and so was I.

We hadn't lost any boats or archers lately; although, Henry had a close call off Tyre—a couple of Tunisian war galleys tried to take his galley to get the gold he was rumoured to be carrying to Cyprus. He said he thought about letting them come along-side and trying to take them—but didn't because his galley was loaded with refugees who would have gotten in the way and he had a skeleton crew with only thirty fighting men. It was a good decision; Henry is one of our best men.

Henry got away without having to fight when one of his two Genoese crossbowmen chanced a long shot and put a lucky bolt straight into the chest of the pirate who seemed to be giving the orders on the nearest galley.

And got three silver coins from Henry for his trouble and three more from William when they reached Cyprus. Henry did even better—he promoted him on the spot to be a "chosen man."

Henry must have made some kind of promise to God or gotten daft from the pressure of the fight because the first thing he did when he got back to Cyprus was to come see me and ask me to marry him up with his lass.

And the marrying sickness spread.

Within the day, Yoram and Lena showed up with the same request and so did the two English widows with a couple of bashful young boat wrights in tow.

We had so many wedding celebrations Andrew Brewer couldn't brew the ale fast enough and we had to buy wine in the city.

****** *Thomas*

William was keeping the men busy while we waited for the return of our last two galleys, and we were almost ready to depart for England.

The four galleys already in the harbour had been loaded with supplies and the sailors and archers who would be sailing on them had been assigned to their places. Similarly, the relocation of the refugees and the tented barracks of the men and workers who will stay was completed.

The hired workers and the refugees and freed slaves who were still with us as churls were now out beyond the second wall along with Brian's fletchers, Tom Cook's kitchen, and the smithy of Alan the smith and his helpers.

Once we sailed for England, only Yoram and his family and the siege supplies would be allowed inside our little fortress; only Henry and his wife and the sergeants who remain will be allowed in the inner courtyard behind the first curtain wall; and only the unmarried archers and apprentice archers who remain will be allowed in the courtyard inside our new outer curtain wall.

It will be Yoram and Henry's most important job to make sure all the doors and gates are constantly barred and guarded to insure the safety of their families and the men who remain.

Both Thomas the cook and Andrew the brewer were coming with us to England. One of the refugees was taking over from Thomas as the sergeant of the kitchen.

The biggest change of all was that the brewing and free ale would end—anyone who wanted a drink after Andrew Brewer left would have to go to one of the wine taverns or ale houses in the city.

To further support the idea there will be no coins in the citadel for thieves and raiders to steal, we did in Limassol what we did in Alexandria—prepaid the local merchants for our food and supplies until the middle of next summer.

The local merchants were pleased with the prepayments and agreed to wait until we returned for any additional payments, which might be due to from whatever Yoram buys while we are gone.

In fact, of course, and even though neither of them knew about the other, both Yoram and Henry were each given more than enough "secret" coins to get everyone through the winter and the following spring.

******

Things were getting more and more hectic for William and me as we got closer and closer to leaving for England. And not everything was going smoothly.

As expected, the boat-wrights recommended the cog be pulled out on to shore to be refreshed and rebuilt. Their plan was to pull it out on the beach and repair it there. It was a fine plan, except it didn't work.

They got the cog out of the water all right and pulled it up on the beach—and then it tipped over and crushed the leg of one of the carpenter's apprentices as it came down. They were still trying to figure out how to right the cog so they could repair the damage.

As we expected, not all the men who made their marks to join us were willing to go with us to England. Already several dozen of them had run, mostly in the distant ports their galleys touched because Cyprus was too small.

England, it seems, is a strange and distant land for the men who were birthed elsewhere. Also, some of the English men-at-arms we recruited in the Holy Land didn't want to become apprentice archers and be learnt to use longbows.

****** *Thomas*

William and I spent much of the time prior to our departure with Harold and the pilots looking at parchment maps and talking about the ports we'd try to visit along the way, and the rendezvous points for when we get separated.

We were trying to be careful because we knew what happened to the girl who became Richard's queen and his sister. It was a close run thing—they should have waited for better weather.

Our plan was to wait until the weather looked good and the winds favourable, which they tended to be this time of year. Then all six of our galleys would hoist their sails and row hard for Rhodes. From Rhodes, we'd hop from port to port on our way to England.

The coins we didn't leave with Yoram and Henry to hide for emergencies were divided between the galleys. There were chests and chests of them. We'd be rich men in England and able to take care of George forever if even one of our galleys gets through.

I would be in Harold's big galley with George and two of the local boys who were being learnt with him. We were sailing with Harold because his galley looked to be the most seaworthy. William would sail in another. Hopefully, by using lanterns at night, we'd be able to stay together all the way to Rhodes and on the sailing legs thereafter as we hop from port to port on our way to England.

After Rhodes, we'd repeat the lantern-using process at night and try to island hop together from Rhodes to the Christian ports of Valletta on Malta and then to Cagliari on the southern end of Sardinia and then to Palma on Mallorca and then past Gibraltar to Lisbon.

With good winds and hard rowing, we hoped to be able to reach Lisbon in ten to twelve days of sailing and four or five days of port visits.

We knew, of course, it was likely to take much longer since we'd be spending time resupplying in the ports we reached, the winds wouldn't always be good, and at each port we'd be waiting for the laggards and lost to catch up and good weather.

The biggest delays, however, would be the raids William intended to conduct against the bases of the Moorish pirates. His plan was to take some of our galleys and men from Malta to Tunis and back to Malta; and from Mallorca to Algiers and back Mallorca.

What William intended to do was breath taking and simple—he intended to sail straight into the Moorish ports as if he owned them, cut out a few prizes, and then row away fast before the Moors had a chance to gather their forces and stop him.

"It'll be like grabbing the honey in a bee's nest and running before the bees have a chance to sting us, won't it?"

After William's raids, we'd do the usual for galley travel— hug the Spanish and French coasts until the weather looked good and we could dash across the channel to a final rendezvous at Falmouth.

Harold thought it would be the safest route and would probably take us about thirty-five days to cover if there were no big storms and we constantly rendezvous and wait a reasonable amount of time for our laggards to come in.

Harold, of course, didn't know about the raids William was planning to make along the way when he made his estimate of how long it would take us to reach England. No one initially knew except William and me. Later, Harold was brought in to help with the planning and the necessary training.

****** *Thomas*

Autumn was coming and tempers were flaring. The atmosphere around our compound in Cyprus got tenser and tenser as the date for our galleys' departure for England got closer and closer.

Yoram and Henry were spending most of their time gathering supplies and doing whatever they could do to speed up the construction projects to make their new families safer.

William, on the other hand, was concentrating on planning the voyage and organising and training the men who would be sailing with us. And he wanted to know what he and his galleys would be going up against, so he talked to every slave and sailor he could find who had ever been to Tunis and Algiers—*how are the harbours laid out? Where are the galleys and boats anchored and pulled ashore?* That sort of thing.

William's emphasis on having the men constantly practise for the trip to England caused Yoram and Henry a great deal of anxiety. They didn't know of his secret plan to raid the ports of the Moorish pirates or they might have been more understanding; as it was, they wanted our men to spend their time working to strengthen our Cyprus defences and were unhappy when they didn't.

Of course, they were anxious; they were the ones whose families would be killed or sold into slavery if our defences didn't hold out until we returned next year.

I talked to William about Yoram and Henry's concerns, but he was adamant. He insisted everyone going to England spend most of their time practising.

For William, strengthening the compound's defences was of lesser importance because the work on Cyprus could continue after we left; what came first for William was practising the destruction of the pirate fleets at Tunis and Algiers without anyone knowing his plans.

I knew William's plans, but he was understandably keeping them secret from everyone else. No one else knew about them except Harold and me.

Improving the defence of our compound and its little two-room citadel, and filling it with enough arrows and water and food supplies to withstand a prolonged siege was what Yoram and Henry were concentrating on with the men who would be staying behind.

Their efforts were not going well.

The new outer curtain wall and its gate and battlements were far from finished despite the fact that we seem to have hired every available man on Cyprus. As a result, Yoram and Henry were seriously worried about the governor or some of his men launching a raid in an effort to steal the coins we'd been earning.

The sad reality was that our defences might not yet be strong enough to defeat a sustained attack or a prolonged siege. In particular, the water well slowly being dug in the inner courtyard had not yet reached water.

William and I repeatedly debated a big question as the time approached for our departure—should we warn off the King's governor or kill him now before he had a chance to act or should we do nothing? Buying him off was not a good way to go because then he'll just keep coming back for more.

On the other hand, if we killed him before we left, the next governor King Guy appointed might be even more dangerous.

William finally reached a conclusion. He decided our best move was to scare the governor enough so he stayed away—so off I went to the governor's castle on the hill above Limassol to do the deed.

****** *Thomas*

King Guy's young governor was one of his new French knights, one of those who only recently came out to replace the knights the King managed to get killed at Hattin. He was rumoured to be a distant cousin of the King or the bastard of someone important in the French court. He seemed to be stupid enough to be either.

Fortunately, the governor was courteous enough or bored enough to immediately receive me in his filthy great hall.

It stinks even more than last time; he must not have a dog to eat the scraps he and his men throw on the floor. We don't have one either, of course, because I insisted. Instead of dogs, we have a refugee woman who picks up the bones and sweeps the dirt floor in our great hall every day as part of her duties.

"Thank you for seeing me so promptly Sir Phillip, ah Governor that is. It's good to see you again. As you may know, Lord William and a few of his archers will soon be off to England for a few months to recruit additional men.

"It is because Lord William will be going to England for a few months that I've come about a sensitive matter – to make sure our compound is not raided while we are gone.

"It won't be the coins the raiders will be after, of course, because we are taking them all with us to England. No, it will be to destroy our compound to discourage us from coming back."

I was trying to gull him—we were not taking all the coins; some would be given to Henry and Yoram for emergencies and many more were buried under the citadel's dirt floor so they'd be available if we have to leave England in a hurry.

I shook my head sadly.

"The raiders, of course, will be making many bad mistakes. Not only will they take terrible losses and find no coins, but Lord William will undoubtedly come back and kill them even if they do get into our citadel. Unfortunately, of course, it will be too late to keep you from being murdered."

The poor man reared his head back and sat up in surprise. He couldn't believe what he had just heard and he certainly didn't understand it.

"What? What did you just say?"

"Oh, I can see by your face that no one's warned you?" I said.

"Well then, it's probably a good thing I've come. Might I ask if you've heard about the Old Man on the mountain and his assassins?"

"Of course," the governor responded warily as he stared at me intently, "everybody has. But it's just a tale."

"Unfortunately, it's not a tale. It's true; very true. The assassins exist; just ask King Guy or any of the men who served with him in Jerusalem. In any event I am here because some of the merchants in Tyre recently paid the Old Man to kill someone right here on Cyprus if our compound is raided— you."

The governor was surprised. Totally surprised. His mouth actually dropped open in shock and disbelief, and then he snapped it shut and irately and loudly demanded to know what in hell I was talking about. *God, he has a foul breath.*

"As you probably know, Governor, one of our galleys just came back from Tyre with a load of refugees. It brought with it information about our danger and yours.

"It seems the merchants who handle Lord William's affairs in Tyre heard a rumour, a false rumour of course. The merchants think someone, probably you, intends to raid our compound while we are gone even if there are no coins there for them to steal.

"In a nutshell, they are worried that if you destroy our post Lord William will decide to quit Cyprus and destroy their chances of escaping the Saracens on his galleys—so they've made arrangements for you to die if anyone conducts a raid or if there are any more rumours about you planning one.

"They think, of course, that you being dead will encourage William to return even if your raid is successful."

It's not true, of course, but that's what I told him. God will forgive me.

The governor was dismayed; the poor fool began anxiously pacing back and forth in front of me. He was totally confused and didn't know whether to be angry or worried or both. It was all I could do not to laugh as I ploughed on.

"Yes, I am afraid it's true," I continued sadly. "The assassins, you know, don't kill their victims directly." *He doesn't know that and neither do I.*

"The way they work is to have someone the victim knows kill him. So if they hear of an attack on our compound, or even of a plan for one, they will merely send a message to someone who knows you such as King Guy or one of your knights— either you kill your governor or we'll kill you.

"It always works, you know, because the man who gets the Old Man's message doesn't want to take a chance of being killed himself. It's how the assassins kill someone without risking themselves."

Finally, the poor fellow found his voice.

"That's impossible," he croaked. "Impossible, I tell you."

"Impossible King Guy won't kill you to save himself? Or someone like his chamberlain won't order you killed to save himself or the King? Think, man. Of course, they'll kill you to save themselves. They know the assassins mean it when they send the ultimatum. Someone always dies."

"But what should I do?"

"Why do nothing, of course—and hope that rumours or news of an attack on Lord William's men never reach the assassins' agent on Cyprus."

Then I pretended to think for a moment.

"There is one thing you could do," I finally suggested. "It would probably save you."

Chapter Twenty-three

Captain William

There were a surprising number of women and children weeping and tearing at their hair on the quay as we rowed out of the Limassol harbour bound for England.

The scene was quite astonishing, actually. But, then again, we had a lot of men on our six galleys—about one hundred and fifty on each and almost all of them sailors and fighting men.

The death of Quick when Harold's prize sunk and the five original archers choosing to stay behind meant only Thomas and I and ten others of the original one hundred and ninety-two archers would be sailing for England.

We left forty archers and men-at-arms with Yoram as well as about thirty men for Henry to train as archers and help defend our fortress and work on strengthening it. We could leave so few because we were taking all five of the governor's knights and twenty of his best men-at-arms to England with us.

A couple of the governor's men were clearly not happy about leaving their families and the warmth of Cyprus, but Sir Phillip didn't give them any choice in the matter. He wasn't taking any chances either—he just gave them their orders and barred the gate to his castle after they left to join us.

Thomas gave him ten gold bezants for their services to help him save face and his priestly word of honour that he and I would do whatever it takes to make sure the Tyre merchants do not send the Old Man's assassins after him.

******

We made good time to Rhodes. When we arrived we found a small harbour with only a few boats in it and a big and seriously undermanned fortress. It was, we were given to understand by the local merchants, ruled somewhat haphazardly by a governor from Constantinople.

Because the nights were clear and moonlit, we were able to stick together all the way to Rhodes. It helped when I deliberately scheduled our departure to start about six days before a full moon and ordered at least two candle lanterns be hung on every mast.

As a result of the moon and the lanterns, all six of our galleys entered Rhodes' harbour at the same time—causing, we came to find out, more than a little anxiety among the townspeople and merchants. They initially thought we might be Tunisian raiders and some of them actually ran to the fortress to take shelter.

We didn't stay long in Rhodes. The weather looked good and the winds favourable—so we quickly replenished our water skins and barrels and departed a few hours later for Crete.

And once again we lost a couple of men. They jumped on to the wharf and ran for it. It was probably a good thing I kept my plans for raiding Algiers and Tunis a secret or even more of them might have run.

Two days later we rowed into Irakleio on the northern side of Crete. Thirty minutes later the clouds moved in and we had the first rain we've seen since we left Cyprus.

It wasn't a big storm. A few hours later the sun returned, and the men were given leave to go ashore to stretch their legs and visit the local taverns and prostitutes.

******

Crete was very much of a seafaring place and we soon attracted a steady stream of men seeking employment as sailors and pilots, and even a few soldiers.

Harold spoke with them and recruited several fishermen who claimed to know the waters between here and Malta. They were willing to make their marks to pilot us to Malta on short-term contracts.

While Harold talked to the local sailors and pilots, I met with the galley captains about their supply needs and twice went into the market with Thomas and my son to fill them. It was a long way to Malta and we needed to be as ready as possible.

******

We left Crete the next morning, but the fact that the moon was full when the sun finished passing over us didn't do us any good at all—we sailed into a storm and the galleys promptly got separated before it even got completely dark.

The result of the storm was inevitable—our galleys straggled into Malta's harbour one at a time over the course of more than a day. When the galley I was on with George and Harold entered the harbour, we found two of our galleys already tied up to one of its long wooden wharves.

******

Malta's harbour was extremely busy, and once again our entrance caused an initial alarm—and rightly so: Algerian and Tunisian war galleys were well-known to the people and sailor men of this part of the world and greatly feared. But, once again, we rowed right in as if we owned the place and peacefully tied up at the old stone quay from which the wharves ran. No one tried to stop us.

I am beginning to get optimistic—I think what I have in mind for Tunis and Algiers might really work.

One of the missing galleys followed us in a couple of hours after we moored. We were beginning to get a bit worried about the last one when it finally showed up the next afternoon—the Greek pilot we'd recruited in Crete hadn't realised he'd steered too far north until he recognised the coastline of Sicily looming ahead of him.

Hopefully, he knows how to find Tunis; he's the pilot on the galley from which I had planned to lead the raid. I may have to rethink my plan.

We had an interesting experience while we were anxiously waiting for the missing galley to arrive—we met Malta's newly installed ruler, Count Brindisi.

Strangely enough, we met him when George got hungry after we visited the market and we stopped at one of the little city's three taverns for something to eat. Count Brindisi was there, of all things, to consult a fortune teller. And he was anxious to hear the latest news from the Holy Land.

The Count was a big, red-faced Greek who had been a rather famous Christian pirate. He had recently gotten himself nobled and given Malta as his fief.

It seems he and his galleys and men helped the current Sicilian King seize the throne when the last of the Hauteville kings died without an heir. Malta was his reward. *There are some lessons to be learnt in that, yes, there are.*

"Why didn't you seize the throne for yourself?" Thomas inquired.

Brindisi's response was quite candid and delivered with a great roaring laugh as he offered fresh grapes to George and the two lads who were accompanying him.

"I didn't have enough men, English, or I certainly would have done."

Then the fortune teller whispered something to him and he gave me a surprised look.

"You're going after a bigger island?"

******

Our galleys took on water and supplies and gathered their crews from the taverns and the city's sole whorehouse. Then all of the galleys, except the one captained by Harold, moved away from the quay and anchored in the harbour. It was Wednesday afternoon.

The men thought we'd be sailing for Lisbon in the morning. We were not. If the weather looked favourable, I'd tell the men our next destination in the morning after we cleared the harbour—and we'd sail directly for Tunis after they found out.

Harold's galley was the biggest and most seaworthy of our six galleys. It was the galley Thomas been on with George and it was where Thomas and George and Harold would wait until I return. It was also where the sergeant captains and sailing sergeants of all our galleys assembled early Thursday morning after Harold moved his galley out into the harbour so we could talk privately.

Harold, to his dismay, did not go on the raid; Thomas insisted he always be the captain of any galley or cog carrying George.

The sergeant captains thought they were coming to get their sailing orders for Lisbon. In fact, they were there so I could explain where we were going next and what they and their men would be expected to do when we got there. I also showed them three big signal flags of different colours and told them what each flag meant if the galley I was on waved it from its mast.

Our meeting lasted for hours and there were many questions, and rightly so, before I finally adjourned it and sent the sergeants back to their galleys to get them ready—with strict orders to keep total silence about our plan. Their crews were not to be told until all five of the galleys going on the raid had cleared the harbour and were on their way to Tunis.

"I knew it," I heard Little Matthew say excitedly to Simon as the two archer sergeants waited for their sailors to come alongside and row them back to the galleys they are commanding.

"I knew all our practicing meant something. I just didn't know what."

******

In a fast galley, Tunis was little more than one day of hard rowing away from Malta and even less if the wind was favourable. Ours were fast and the wind looked good.

After the meeting with my captains and their sergeants, I gave George a big kiss and hug, shook my brother's hand as we gave each other a hug, and patted each other on the back, and moved to Archie's galley with my signal flags.

An Arab-speaking former slave came with me. He'd act as my translator if I needed one—which I almost certainly would if I were able to find a Tunisian fishing boat.

I left Thomas and Harold with somewhat of a skeleton crew. *They would have to recruit more rowers locally if we didn't return.*

Tunis and all the shoreline of Africa and Spain, from here to beyond Gibraltar and all the way to Lisbon, were ruled by the Almohad king and his heathen Berbers. The sailors call it the Berber Coast or the Barbary Coast.

Whatever it's called, it's a dangerous place for a Christian or Jew. That's because its Moorish king gets the coins he spends on his wars from the taking and selling of slaves. In other words, it would not do at all to have the Berbers in Tunis learn we were coming to pay them a visit.

That's why our five galleys were anchored close together in the middle of the harbour and our men were not allowed to set foot on shore to talk in the taverns and whorehouses.

******

Five galleys sailed Thursday morning as Thomas, George, and Harold waved goodbye. I'd moved from Harold's galley to Archie's after I met with the sergeants. Archie's a former serf from Sussex and one of the original archers. John from Dover was his pilot and the sergeant of his sailors.

We stayed close together all that day and the moonlit night that followed. The moon gave our pilots our location and the African coast near Tunis was in sight when the sun came up Friday morning.

The first thing I did as the sun came up and began passing over us was seek out a fishing boat to get the prayer times for tomorrow at Tunis. The galley captains knew I planned to do this if we came upon a fishing boat, and why. So they slowed down and waited, but did not follow me, when I peeled off towards one of the fishing boats in the fishing fleet we came upon as we entered the Gulf of Tunis.

The three men on the fishing boat we approached initially thought we were a galley out of Tunis and scarcely paid any attention to us at all; at least, not until we got within hailing distance and our translator began asking them about the times of prayer.

A few minutes of friendly conversation between the fishermen and the translator turned to me with a smile.

"Tomorrow is Friday, the big day of prayers in Tunis. The most important prayers will start at high noon, and then again just after sundown. And would we like to buy some fresh fish?"

We had made a fast passage and arrived off Tunis too early. So I ordered the rowers to stop and hoisted the "form on me" flag.

******

About two hours passed after I finished speaking with the fishermen. Then an Arab dhow came past us heading for the harbour entrance. It concerned me greatly because of the possibility the sailors on the dhow might raise the alarm—so I ordered the "follow me" flag to be waved from the mast and off we rowed to follow the dhow to Tunis.

All five of our galleys rowed as fast as possible straight through the Tunis harbour entrance. Archie's galley, the one I was on, led the way. We sped through the many boats at anchor in the harbour at our best speed and headed straight for the Tunisian galleys.

Some of them were moored to the quay, but most of them were nosed into the strand next to the walled city's quay and secured from drifting away by a line from their bow to a mooring post on the shore—exactly where and how we expected to find them.

Archie did what he was told and headed towards the beach with the other galleys following close behind.

There were a few men loitering about on the beach and on the decks of the Tunisian galleys, but not many. It was Friday, the Muslim Sabbath, and most of their crewmen were apparently sleeping or in the city for Friday prayers.

The loitering men watched as we approached and backed our oars as we coasted up to the shoreline. They didn't even begin to run until our men poured off our galleys and began to wade ashore carrying their shields and swords. Not a one of them stayed to fight.

That's when all of our hours of practise paid off. Swords cut through mooring lines and the designated prize crews scrambled aboard as a mass of willing hands began pushing the pirate galleys backwards into the water.

It seemed to be taking forever, but within two minutes of our first setting foot on the beach we had prize crews on a dozen or more of the Tunisian galleys.

There was no serious resistance. The Arabs who had been on the galleys for one reason or another and didn't run were instantly cut down as our prize crews swarmed aboard. They were left wherever they fell in the rush to get the captured galleys underway.

Almost immediately the slave-rowed oars of our prizes turned them around and began to row them out of the harbour. Our prize crews were organised under an experienced sergeant and each had an Arab-speaking translator to give orders to the galley slaves chained to their rowing benches.

Archie's galley did not go all the way in to the beach with the others. Instead, we temporarily took up a blocking position in case any of the pirate galleys in the harbour or beached along the shoreline were manned and decided to come out and fight.

It was immediately obvious we'd caught the Tunisians totally by surprise and totally unready to fight. So I ordered Archie to row for the quay as soon as I saw the men of our prize crews begin to jump into the shallow water and head for the beached galleys.

Our galleys, once the men of their prize crews reached the beach and their prizes were in the water, quickly turned around and headed towards the cogs and other cargo boats anchored in the harbour. They were to either burn the Moorish transports or tow them away as prizes—and they were to keep at it until I flew the recall flag. Then they were to sail back to Malta.

Within minutes, our galleys were hard at work burning and seizing the boats in the harbour, and the Tunisian galleys our prize crews seized on the beach were rowing for Malta at the best possible speeds their slave rowers and our prize crews could provide.

Archie's galley did not immediately join the others in going after the cargo boats anchored in the harbour. We headed straight for the quay in front of the city and the cogs and dhows moored along it.

All along the deck on the shore side of our galley, boarding parties were standing grouped together around their sergeant— six of them. Each consisted of nine or ten axe-men, archers, and shield-carrying swordsmen carrying bundles of dried twigs and lighted lanterns.

On the other side of the deck were our best longbow archers. Once the boarding parties were on the quay, the archers moved across to the shore side of our galley and lined the deck railing to provide cover for them.

And that's what happened. As soon as Archie's galley bumped up against the quay, our six boarding parties poured over the galley railing and began running along the quay to get to the cogs and galleys moored all along it.

Each boarding party on the quay or on the strand had two alternatives for each galley it boarded.

The first alternative was to board a galley with no slaves to act as rowers, light it on fire and cut its mooring lines and push it away from the quay so it could not be re-boarded and the fire put out—and then move to the next galley and repeat the process over and over again until they either ran out of possible prizes or the recall flag went up on my galley.

As you might imagine, only the sergeant leading the boarding party was authorised to light the fire and cut the mooring lines. I promised to hang any man who cut or cast off a mooring line and stranded a fire lighter or any of our men on an enemy galley with no slaves to row it to Malta—and I certainly meant it. It was in the company's contract that no man would be left behind.

The second alternative was much better than the first—board a galley with slaves chained to its rowing benches, put down the men defending it, and then cut it loose and stay aboard as a prize crew—and have the slaves row it to Malta as a prize instead of setting it on fire.

For the first few minutes everything went according to plan. The only opposition initially came from a few of the surprised and easily overwhelmed sailors our boarding parties found on the galleys they boarded.

But then the inevitable occurred—men who had seen the galleys being taken on the beach ran to the city and sounded the alarm.

Suddenly, a few and then hundreds and then thousands of shouting men, mostly unarmed, thank God, appeared almost out of nowhere and came running out of the city and down towards the quay—and were met by a shower of arrows as I hoisted the recall flag and our boarding parties rushed back to my galley.

It's a good thing we had the archers ready and the Moors go into their mosques without weapons; one of our boarding parties spent too much time starting a fire and had to fight its way back to join us. That's when one of our men was killed and several wounded.

******

The arrow storm continued until the last of our boarding parties climbed back on to Archie's galley and we began moving through the smoke towards the boats and galleys anchored nearby in the harbour.

I don't think our galley captains left anyone behind. I hope not; the Moors seemed quite upset as we pushed off and rowed away—there was lots of shouting and many fists being shaken.

We reached the first of the cogs and other cargo transports anchored in the harbour soon after our other galleys got among them after attacking the Tunisian galleys on the beach.

All of our galleys followed the same process—grapple a likely-looking boat, board it and kill everyone who resisted, and then either light it on fire or leave a few men on board as a prize crew if it had slave rowers. My galley burned a couple of cogs and sent a Tunisian galley towards Malta as a prize.

Then I really make a big mess of things when I had Archie send a boarding party on a big cog and we tried to tow it out of the harbour. The damn tow line came loose, and we wasted precious minutes futilely trying to retie it.

Finally, I gave up and we came back alongside, re-boarded the men of Archie's boarding party, and followed our other galleys and their prizes out of the harbour. The cog we could not tow, so far as I could see, was the only one in the harbour not burning or being towed out as a prize.

It was quite embarrassing actually; particularly since the galley we followed out of the harbour was towing the biggest three-masted dhow I'd ever seen.

******

Three of our original galleys, including the one I was on, spent the rest of the day waiting off Tunis as a blocking force to give our prizes and the galley towing the big dhow time to get further away from Tunis and reduce the possibility of them being retaken.

To everyone's surprise not a single Moorish galley came out of Tunis to try to retake our prizes, at least we didn't see any.

Finally, as the sun was setting, I had the "follow me" flag waved from our mast and our little group of three galleys began slowly making its way back to Malta; hopefully keeping our galleys between our prizes and any pissed off Tunisians who might come out to try to retake them.

The weather was good and we stayed together most of the way; the only sails we saw, and ignored, were a couple of Spanish cogs, which appeared to be bound for Malta.

Chapter Twenty-four

Captain William

All of the men and slaves on our prizes were deathly afraid of being taken by the Tunisians, and rightly so. So it was little wonder they rowed for Malta like the devil himself was breathing on the back of their necks.

As a result, many of our prizes were already tied up and taking on water and supplies when we rowed into the harbour. Most of the rest straggled in over the next twenty-four hours. But not all of them.

After almost a week of waiting, we were still missing several prizes and their prize crews. No one had any idea where they might be or why they did not make it back to Malta.

Maybe they lost their bearings and would show up later; maybe the Moors somehow got past our blocking force with their surviving galleys and retook them; maybe their crews decided to desert.

The possibilities were endless, and we would most likely never know.

We ended up reaching Malta with seventeen new galleys, two cogs, and a large, ocean-going Arab dhow. The dhow had three masts and lateen sails none of our sailors know how to use. Our losses were three men killed, a dozen or so wounded, and twenty-six missing.

We also came away with about eight hundred malnourished slaves whom we promptly freed and put on double rations to strengthen them up for the hard days ahead as we rowed to England.

About half of the slaves were black Africans and Arabs; the other half were mostly Christian and Jewish sailors including forty or so ecstatically happy British and French, some of whom had been slaves of the Tunisians for many years.

Well over four hundred of the slaves accepted our offer to carry them to England via Lisbon and the coast of France. The rest apparently wanted to keep their feet on dry land for a while.

******

My plans were changed by the size of our success. We didn't have enough men to fully crew all of our prizes, so we were not going to visit Algiers and try to fetch even more, at least not on this trip.

There was no doubt about it, we had taken so many prizes we'd be several hundred rowers short, even if all the former slaves volunteered to come with us—which they certainly wouldn't.

As a result, our unexpectedly big problem was to decide which prizes to keep and what to do with those we couldn't take with us because we didn't have enough men to crew them.

In the end, we decided to sail some of our new galleys shorthanded and keep all of our prizes except the big Arab dhow; it would take too many of our skilled seamen to handle its sails.

The only exception to the galley and cogs, which would be going out shorthanded, was the big galley carrying George and my brother and about half of our coin chests—it would sail with Harold as its captain and a full crew of our best and strongest sailors and men-at-arms including me and Thomas.

*****

We waited for almost a week for the last two stragglers and then two more days for good weather. While we waited, we provisioned our boats and more than two hundred of the slaves who initially wanted to stay ashore changed their minds and joined us to get food and shelter and stay away from the local slave catchers.

It probably helped when some of the slaves talked to the men in our crews we'd already freed from slavery and learnt they really would be fed and become free churls if they join us.

Nine days after our raid on Tunis, we sailed for England after selling the dhow to a local merchant for a fraction of its value. We also made arrangements for the crews of our stragglers to be cared for and sheltered if they arrived and were not in condition to follow us.

Twenty-one galleys and two cogs left Malta bright and early on a Sunday morning. Four days later, we began arriving in the harbour of Palma on the island of Mallorca. Five days later we sailed for Lisbon.

*****

Our fleet pretty much stayed together as we rowed past the Moorish ports along the Spanish coast. The good weather lasted until we passed through the narrows at Gibraltar and entered the Atlantic.

Then the weather turned bad and separated us. Every galley and cog was on its own as we turned north for the run past the Moors at Cadiz and on to Lisbon.

It was a hot and sunny, early autumn day, and we were running low on water when we finally rowed into the great harbour at Lisbon eight days later.

Only three of our boats had arrived before us, including, to everyone's surprise, one of the cogs. It had somehow ridden the winds of the storm all the way from Gibraltar to Lisbon. Most of the rest straggled into the harbour in the days that followed.

Almost a week later, the winds and the weather look good enough to leave. That's when the "follow me" flag was waved and Harold's galley led the seventeen boats of our fleet out of the Lisbon harbour including both cogs.

Bob the tailor and his galley were the only ones who stayed behind. He'd wait for another week or so and organise the five stragglers if and when they arrived.

Thirteen days later, Thomas and I stood on the deck with George and looked at the coast of Cornwall looming as a low grey mass in the distance.

"There it is, George, England. That's your home."

—End of Book One —

Please read more. The rest of the action-packed books in this great saga of medieval England are all available on Kindle as eBooks and some are available in print. You can find them by going to your Amazon website and searching for *Martin Archer fiction.* A collection of the first six books is available on Kindle as *The Archers' Story.* Similarly, a collection of the next four novels in the saga is available as *The Archers' Story: Part II,* and there are additional books beyond those four.

Martin hopes you enjoyed reading *The Archers.* If so, he respectfully requests a favourable review on Amazon and elsewhere with as many stars as possible in order to encourage other readers. He can be reached at martinarcherV@gmail.com

Amazon eBooks in the exciting and action-packed *The Company of Archers* saga:

The Archers

The Archer's Castle

The Archer's War

The Archer's Return

Rescuing the Hostages

Kings and Crusaders

The Archers' Gold

The Missing Treasure

Castling the King

The Sea Warriors

The Captain's Men

Gulling the Kings

The Archers' Magna Carta

Amazon eBooks in Martin Archer's exciting and action-packed *Soldier and Marines* saga:

Soldier and Marines

Peace and Conflict

War Breaks Out

War in the East

Israel's Next War

Collections

The Archer's Story - books I, II, III, IV, V, VI

The Archer's Story II - books VII, VIII, IX, X,

Soldiers and Marines Trilogy

Other eBooks you might enjoy:

Cage's Crew by Martin Archer writing as Raymond Casey

America's Next War by Michael Cameron

Made in the USA
San Bernardino, CA
14 October 2017